THE CLUE OF THE LEANING CHIMNEY

AS a result of an encounter with a sinister stranger on a lonely country road, Nancy Drew and her friend Bess Marvin discover that a rare and valuable Chinese vase has been stolen from the pottery shop of Dick Milton, a cousin of Bess.

Dick had borrowed the vase from his Chinese friend, elderly Mr. Soong. He is determined to repay Mr. Soong for the loss and tells Nancy that if he can find "the leaning chimney," he feels he will be on the track of a discovery which will solve his financial problems.

Nancy finds the leaning chimney, but it only leads her into more puzzles. Can there be any connection between the vase theft—one of a number of similar crimes—and the strange disappearance of the pottery expert Eng Moy and his daughter Lei?

Join Nancy and her friends in their exciting adventures as they unravel all the twisted strands of this intriguing mystery.

*A man was stepping through a panel in the
rear of the closet*

The Clue of the Leaning Chimney

BY CAROLYN KEENE

GROSSET & DUNLAP
Publishers • New York
A member of The Putnam & Grosset Group

Copyright © 1995, 1967, 1949 by Simon & Schuster, Inc. All rights reserved.
Published by Grosset & Dunlap, Inc., a member of The Putnam &
Grosset Group, New York. Published simultaneously in Canada. Printed in the U.S.A.
NANCY DREW MYSTERY STORIES® is a registered trademark of Simon & Schuster,
Inc. **GROSSET & DUNLAP** is a trademark of Grosset & Dunlap, Inc.
Library of Congress Catalog Card Number: 67-20845 ISBN 978-0-448-09526-4

Contents

The Clue
of the
Leaning Chimney

CHAPTER I

The Mysterious Stranger

"Oh, Nancy, this road is so lonely! And here we are with all this money. It'd be awful if it were stolen!"

Bess Marvin gripped the handbag in her lap a bit more tightly and peered nervously through the windshield of the convertible.

A dark forest flowed past the car on either side of the road. Black clouds were gathering in the night sky, and the wind whispered dismally through the swaying trees.

The pretty, somewhat plump girl shivered slightly.

"Cheer up, Bess," comforted the slim, titian-haired driver. "We'll soon be home."

Nancy Drew spoke with more confidence than she felt. As she deftly steered the car around a turn in Three Bridges Road, her blue eyes mirrored a slight uneasiness in her own thoughts. She glanced at the handbag in Bess's lap. It contained three hundred and forty-two dollars and sixty-three cents, the proceeds of a charity rummage sale the two eighteen-year-old girls had run that evening in Masonville.

Nancy, who was treasurer of the group, had the responsibility of depositing the money in a River Heights bank. Studying the dark, deserted road ahead, she wondered if she had not made a mistake in taking the lonely short cut. The attractive girl tucked a stray wisp of hair into place and put the thought firmly out of her mind.

"Don't be a ninny," she chided herself. "Just because there's no traffic, that's no reason to start imagining things."

"Nancy, can't you drive faster?" Bess asked.

Stealing a look at her nervous companion, Nancy smiled with affection. Bess was one of her closest friends.

There was a sudden flash of lightning, followed by a clap of thunder. A few drops of rain spattered against the windshield.

"Oh dear!" wailed Bess. "More trouble."

Nancy did not comment. The car was approaching a series of sharp, twisting curves in the road just this side of Hunter's Bridge. Driving safely around them required all her attention.

As they rounded the final turn, the headlights suddenly focused on a man. He was bending over something in the road, directly in the path of the car! He was unaware of Nancy's car!

The man was unaware of Nancy's car!

Bess screamed. Nancy twisted the steering wheel frantically, at the same time jamming her wrist against the horn and stepping on the brake. There was a screech of tires as the car swerved past the man and came to a stop thirty feet beyond.

"D-did we—?" Bess stuttered, unable to speak the awful thought that they had hit the man.

Nancy quickly took a flashlight from the front compartment and got out of the car. The man was lying in the middle of the road!

"Oh, Bess!" she cried fearfully. "He's hurt!"

But even as she hurried toward him, the man stumbled to his feet and began looking around him in the road as if he had lost something.

"Are you all right? I didn't hurt you?" Nancy asked.

To her astonishment he growled, "Go away!"

The brim of his battered felt hat was pulled low over his forehead and the turned-up collar of his topcoat concealed his mouth and chin. But Nancy got a quick glimpse of a pair of piercing, black eyes. Abruptly the man ran across the road and ducked behind some bushes.

"Is this what you're looking for?" Nancy called, picking up a bundle which had rolled off to one side.

"Put that bundle down and get out of here!" he ordered sharply.

"But I want to help," Nancy protested. "You may be hurt—"

"Listen, sister, I'm okay," his rough voice cut in. "But if you don't go now, *you'll* get hurt!"

As if to emphasize the threat, a rock, hurled out of the darkness, struck the road a scant six inches away and bounded into the ditch.

Bess, who had come up behind Nancy, tugged at her friend's sleeve. "Come on!" she whispered nervously. "He means it!"

But Nancy, her suspicions aroused, turned over the bundle she was holding. As she stared through a large tear in the paper, another rock, well aimed this time, smashed Nancy's flashlight. It also shattered Nancy's chance of getting a better look at the stranger's bundle.

Bess uttered a squeak of fear. "Oh, Nancy, hurry! Put that thing down and come on!"

This time Nancy obeyed the warning and hurried back to the car. Rain was falling in large drops as she started the motor. Nancy looked back, but neither the man nor the bundle was in sight.

"Whew!" said Bess as they drove through the downpour. "Next time you stop to talk to a man on a deserted road, count me out!"

Nancy laughed. "He certainly was nasty," she agreed. "Too bad we couldn't get a good look at him."

"What do you suppose was in that old bundle that made him act so funny?" Bess asked.

"A vase," Nancy told her. "At least, from what I could see, it looked like one. Green porcelain with an enormous red claw."

"Green porcelain with a red claw?" Bess repeated. "That's odd."

"Why?"

"Well, it sounds an awful lot like a vase on display in the window of Dick Milton's pottery shop," Bess went on. "Dick's vase is green, too, and it has a black Chinese dragon with red claws!"

Dick Milton was a cousin of Bess's. He had a small shop on Bedford Street in River Heights where he made and sold pottery. The young man also held classes in ceramics, one of which Bess was attending.

"The vase is beautiful," Bess went on. "Dick didn't make it—somebody lent it to him, I think."

Bess babbled on, explaining the perfection of the vase with the enthusiasm of one who has just learned how various pottery pieces are made.

"You ought to join our class," she said. "It's lots of fun."

Nancy found her attention wandering. Her thoughts went back to the man in the road. What was he doing in such a deserted place so late at night? Obviously he had not wanted to be seen. Her car, suddenly rounding a curve, had caught him unawares. And why had he behaved so strangely about the vase? Could it, by any chance, be the one from Dick Milton's shop?

"Why, Nancy, you're not even listening!" Bess's voice broke in accusingly.

"I'm sorry, Bess," she apologized. "I was thinking of that man and how suspiciously he acted."

"I know what that means," Bess declared. "You're itching for a new mystery to solve!"

Nancy, the daughter of a prominent criminal lawyer, was well known for her ability as an amateur detective. People who were in trouble frequently came to her for assistance.

The rain had ceased and a few stars began to flicker as Nancy drove through River Heights. When she turned into Bedford Street, Bess noted their new direction with surprise.

"This is the way to Dick's shop!"

"I know," said Nancy. "I want to look at his window."

Soon she eased the convertible to a stop under a street lamp in front of the pottery shop. The two girls got out and hurried to the plate-glass window.

Nancy frowned with anxiety as she peered at the clay dishes and bowls displayed on a black velvet background. There was no vase. Nancy tried the door. It was locked.

"The dragon vase has been stolen!" Bess whispered.

"Let's not jump to conclusions," said Nancy as she tried to quell her own fears. "Perhaps Dick put the vase somewhere else for the night. I'll phone him to make sure."

They walked quickly down the street to a corner drugstore. Nancy slipped into a telephone booth and dialed Dick's number. A sleepy hello answered.

"Dick Milton?" asked Nancy. "This is Nancy Drew. I'm sorry to call you so late, but it's urgent."

"What's the matter?" Dick asked excitedly.

"It's about the dragon vase in your store window," replied Nancy. "It isn't there now. Did you remove it?"

"The dragon vase? No!" Dick Milton's voice trembled with emotion. "It was there when I closed the shop. You say it isn't there now? This is terrible!"

"I'll get the police," Nancy offered.

"Tell them," Dick gasped, "the vase doesn't belong to me—and it's worth thousands of dollars!"

CHAPTER II

A Double Theft

DICK said he would come right down. He arrived as a police car pulled up to the curb and two officers stepped out. Nodding to the girls and the police, the young proprietor unlocked the shop door and entered. He switched on the light.

"You say a vase has been stolen?" queried Officer Murphy.

"What kind of vase?" his partner put in quickly.

"A Chinese vase," Dick replied dejectedly. "A rare Ming piece over two thousand years old."

"Whew!" exclaimed Murphy. "Let's see where the thief entered. It's evident it wasn't by the front door."

"Then we'd better check the back," the other officer said.

The two policemen hurried to the rear of the building, followed by Dick, Nancy, and Bess.

"Look!" Murphy exclaimed, pointing to an open window in the back of the shop. Marks of a jimmy were visible on the sill.

"Don't touch anything," Officer Reilly said to Dick, who reached up to close the window. "We'll take fingerprints."

Quickly he opened his kit and dusted the sill and a nearby chair which the thief might have touched as he entered. But not a print was to be found.

"The thief must have worn gloves," Nancy whispered to Dick.

"No doubt he left footprints outside," declared Murphy.

Nancy hurried out the back door with the officers, who beamed their flashlights on the earth beneath the window. Big, oval prints indicated the thief's feet had been covered with something to keep them from making shoe prints.

"What's your guess, Miss Drew?" Murphy asked.

"The thief tied burlap bags over his shoes."

"And I think you're right."

Suddenly they were startled by a cry from Dick, who had gone back to the shop. They ran inside.

"What's the matter?" Nancy asked.

"The small, green jade elephant!" he exclaimed. "It's gone, too!"

"Oh dear!" Bess cried out. "Was that loaned to you, too?"

"Yes," moaned Dick. "It was another of Mr. Soong's pieces. How can I ever repay him!"

"Who's Mr. Soong?" asked Reilly.

"He's a retired Chinese importer who lent me the vase and the elephant," explained Dick. "Business hasn't been so good, so Mr. Soong let me display his pieces, hoping they would attract customers to the shop."

"They attracted more than customers," put in Murphy. "And not a clue to the thief."

"Maybe I have a clue," Nancy spoke up.

Often she stumbled upon a mystery as she had this one. The first case the young sleuth had solved was *The Secret of the Old Clock*. Recently she had unraveled a mystery involving *The Ghost of Blackwood Hall*.

Nancy told the police about the man and the green vase with the large red claw she had seen at Hunter's Bridge.

"He just might be our thief," said Murphy. "Come on, Reilly. Let's try to track him down. Thanks for the tip, Miss Drew."

After the officers had gone, Bess asked Dick when he was going to tell Mr. Soong about the loss.

Dick groaned. "That, Bess, will be the hardest part. And after all Mr. Soong has done for me!"

With leaden feet he walked to the telephone and dialed. The shop was strangely quiet as the three waited for someone to answer at the other end of the line.

"I guess Mr. Soong is either out or asleep," said Dick. "I'll phone him first thing tomorrow morning. Well, it's late," he added. "You girls had better go home."

"If the police don't catch the thief," said Nancy as Dick locked the pottery shop, "I'd like to help you solve the mystery. I'll drop in to see you tomorrow."

The next morning, when Nancy went down to breakfast, her head was still full of the stolen vase mystery. Hannah Gruen, the Drews' middle-aged housekeeper, noticed Nancy's preoccupation as she came from the kitchen carrying a breakfast tray. Mrs. Gruen put the food in front of Nancy, but the girl didn't seem to see it. She sat as if in a trance.

"Wake up, Nancy," the housekeeper said, laughing.

"Oh, Hannah," Nancy said with a smile. "I was just thinking about dragons." She went on to relate the previous night's adventure.

"How strange!" Mrs. Gruen remarked. "But please eat, dear."

Nancy's mother had died many years ago, and the housekeeper had run the Drew household for so long she was regarded as one of the family.

Mrs. Gruen was proud of the young detective's accomplishments, but she always worried when Nancy was working on a case.

Nancy ate quickly and rose from the table. "I must go to Dick Milton's right away," she announced.

On the way, Nancy deposited the rummage-sale money at the bank. When she arrived at the pottery shop, she found the young man in better spirits.

"I told Mr. Soong about the theft first thing this morning," he said. "He was very calm about it all and said that unfortunately the loss was only partly covered by insurance. Of course money can't replace such a rare, old piece. I must somehow repay the part not covered by insurance."

"Any report from the police?" Nancy asked.

"No trace of the thief," Dick answered. "I guess you'd better join in the hunt. But first, will you please do me a favor, Nancy?"

"Surely."

"I want you to take this piece of jewelry back to Mr. Soong. I've explained to him who you are."

Nancy inspected the sea-green jade pendant that Dick held in his palm.

"It's lovely," said Nancy. "May I hold it?"

Dick placed the pendant in her hand. "It's the last piece from Mr. Soong in the shop," Dick explained. "I don't want this to be stolen, too!"

"Oh, I'd be thrilled to take it to Mr. Soong. I've heard his home is like a museum," replied Nancy. "I'd love to meet Mr. Soong, too, and have him tell me about the vase and the elephant. Then, if I ever see his prize possessions, I'll be able to recognize them."

Dick placed the jade on top of a fluff of cotton in a tiny white box, wrapped it, and gave the package to Nancy. Ten minutes later she arrived at the address Dick had given her and parked her car in front of the attractive Colonial house.

She went up the walk, and lifting the brass knocker, rapped on the door. It was opened by a short, inscrutable-looking Chinese servant wearing a black alpaca jacket. He regarded Nancy silently.

"Is Mr. Soong at home?" she inquired.

He bowed slightly and stepped back to let her pass. Nancy waited in the foyer while he closed the door, then he showed her into a study and motioned for her to be seated.

Nancy sat down on a nearby couch and turned to thank the servant, but he had silently disappeared. Her eyes wandered over the study.

As she gazed at the fireplace, her attention became fixed on a square piece of tapestry hung over the mantel. Nancy rose and studied the tapestry more closely. It was richly woven, with a Chinese dragon embroidered in black and red against a background of jade green.

"Do you like it?" a soft voice behind her inquired.

Nancy whirled sharply. Standing in the doorway was a short, gentle-faced Chinese with spectacles and a tiny goatee. He wore a richly brocaded mandarin coat and beautifully embroidered Chinese slippers. His eyes twinkled, and his slippers shuffled softly as he advanced into the study.

"I hope I did not frighten you."

Nancy smiled. "I'm afraid you did, just for a moment! You're Mr. Soong?"

"Yes."

"I'm Nancy Drew, a friend of Dick Milton's."

"Oh yes, the illustrious Drew family. I've heard of you and your father. Please sit down."

After giving him the package, Nancy mentioned last night's robbery. She told Mr. Soong about the strange man on the road. Mr. Soong showed intense interest when she mentioned the dragon's-foot design on the vase.

"This tapestry you found so fascinating," he said, indicating the cloth over the mantel, "bears the identical design that is glazed on the vase."

He rose and went to the fireplace. "The dragon you see here was an emperor's emblem. It has five claws. Only the emperor and his sons and Chinese princes of the first and second rank were allowed to have emblems showing dragons with five claws. Lesser princes had to be content with four-clawed dragons."

"How interesting!" Nancy murmured.

Soong fixed his gentle eyes on Nancy. "Did you notice the number of claws on the vase?"

"No, I didn't," Nancy admitted. She stood up. "I must go now. I'll let you know if I find another clue."

Mr. Soong nodded and smiled. "It was good of you to come," he said in his soft, musical voice. "I have heard much about your detective abilities and I am flattered that one so charming and capable should wish to help me recover the vase." He paused. "Perhaps you can aid me in still another matter, Miss Drew—you and your father."

"What sort of matter is it, Mr. Soong? I'd like to be of service in any way I can, but if it's a legal problem Dad will know how to solve it better than I."

Mr. Soong hesitated. "To tell the truth, I am not certain at this moment what kind of problem it is, although it has legal aspects. Suppose I call on Mr. Drew and tell him about it." His eyes twinkled. "With the condition, of course, that he repeat the story to you."

Nancy laughed. "That's the kind of condition I like!"

Mr. Soong tinkled a tiny Chinese bell and the servant silently appeared.

"Ching will show you out," the elderly Chinese gentleman said. "Good-by."

Nancy returned to Dick's shop and told him

of her visit. "Mr. Soong's a fine person," she added.

"He certainly is," Dick replied, stroking his chin thoughtfully. "That's why I want to repay him as soon as possible. It probably will take a long time," he commented forlornly. "The vase and elephant were worth an awful lot of money."

"I'm going to hunt for them," Nancy said with determination.

"But if you don't find them, I'll pay Mr. Soong back somehow," Dick declared. "I must! And I'm sure I could do it if only—"

His fist hit the top of the counter so hard that the little clay dishes jumped. "If only I could find the leaning chimney!" he exclaimed.

"The leaning chimney?" Nancy asked quizzically. "What's that?"

"I wish I knew." Dick frowned. "It's a clue to some valuable clay. The leaning chimney may be part of a house, part of a factory—or it may exist only in someone's imagination.

"I learned of it by accident. I was in a phone booth one day when I overheard a man talking in the adjoining booth. I didn't pay any attention until I heard 'unusual China clay,' then 'Masonville' and 'leaning chimney.' I tried to hurry my call so I could ask him about the clay, but when I hung up he had disappeared."

Dick sighed. "I've hunted for such a chimney in what little time I could take away from the shop, but all the chimneys I've seen are as straight as a flagpole!"

Nancy laughed, then grew serious once more. "China clay is the main ingredient for making fine pottery, isn't it, Dick?"

"It's the best there is!" he replied. "Why, if I could locate a valuable deposit of China clay nearby, I might buy it cheap, and make the finest of porcelains like the ancient Chinese! Then I could repay Mr. Soong!"

Dick's eyes glowed at the prospect and the worried frown vanished from his face. Seeing the change in him, Nancy determined to do everything in her power to locate the valuable pit.

"Maybe I can help you find the clay, Dick," she said. "I'll try, anyway."

He stared at her in surprise for a moment, then his mouth broke into a wide grin. "Would you?" he exclaimed. "That's mighty swell of you!"

"If what you overheard the man say is true," said Nancy, "the chimney must be somewhere in or around Masonville."

"If it only were!" There was a dreamlike look in Dick's eyes. "I'd enlarge my place, install extra kilns, and do a thriving business. I can just visualize it all—Dick Milton, Inc., Fine Potteries."

Then he smiled. "Please forgive me for such silly daydreaming. But, you see, I would like my wife and baby daughter to be proud of me."

"A little girl? How nice," Nancy said with a smile. "How old is she?"

With a fatherly air of authority he said, beaming, "Susan's her name and she's fifteen months. I'd like you to see her, and meet my wife Connie, too, sometime."

"I'd love to," said Nancy. "But, right now, before I start for Masonville to look for the leaning chimney and the China clay, I'd like to learn more about how you make pottery."

Dick led Nancy into the workroom back of the shop, where the thief had jimmied the window.

In the center of the room stood two long benches crowded with plaster of Paris molds, unfinished clay pieces, a potter's wheel and various jars and cans. Stacked in a corner were huge, round crocks. Dick explained that these contained ordinary moist clay which he had prepared for his classes.

"But one can get much finer results with China clay," he remarked.

"What are those big black boxes?" Nancy asked, pointing to three square, ovenlike vaults on benches to one side of the room.

"Oh, they're my electric kilns for baking." Dick smiled. "I'm firing a piece now. I'll let you have a preview."

He led Nancy over to one kiln. Through a small peephole, she could see a bright-red glow.

Inside was a small pyramid-shaped object and beyond that was a vase about seven inches high.

"This is the biscuit stage," Dick informed her. "When that little cone which you see in front of the vase starts to bend, I'll know my piece is finished and turn off the heat. After the vase is completely cool, I'll put on a coat of glaze and refire it. Then it will be ready for sale."

As Nancy and Dick returned to the front of the shop, she thanked him for his instructive demonstration.

"Bess wants me to join your class," Nancy remarked. "Maybe I will—after I find the leaning chimney!"

At that moment a customer entered the store, and Nancy said good-by.

"Keep me posted," Dick called as she went out.

Nancy walked to her car and started off. As it rolled along the road toward Masonville, she tried to figure out what a leaning chimney would have to do with a clay pit. Perhaps the man whom Dick had overheard was talking about two different things. Maybe there was no link at all between them!

"I may be on a wild-goose chase," Nancy thought. "But it's worth the try."

Almost without realizing it, she found herself on the back road which she and Bess had taken the night before from Masonville. Nearing Hunter's Bridge, she slowed down, then stopped at the side of the road.

"I'll look around," she decided. "Maybe I'll find some kind of clue to the thief's identity."

Sliding across the seat of the convertible, she stepped onto the soft dirt shoulder of the road. The earth was still slightly damp after the rain. Various sizes of heavy shoe marks here and there indicated to Nancy that the police had made an investigation.

Nancy walked into the underbrush a few feet, searching carefully for anything the officers might have overlooked. As she ducked under a bush, a large drop of water slid from its leafy cup and dripped onto her neck. Nancy hunched her shoulders as a chill ran down her back.

Suddenly she heard a faint rustling. Behind the shrubbery a thorny bush with long, prickly branches was quivering violently, as if a moment before someone had brushed against it.

Her breath coming quickly, Nancy glanced at the damp ground behind the bush. Clearly imprinted in the soft earth were a man's footprints!

Was she about to come face to face with the thief who had stolen the vase?

CHAPTER III

The Secret Panel

NANCY advanced a few steps, then stopped to listen. She might hear the thief, she figured, if he were lurking in the woods. But the only sound in the ominously silent thicket was the sudden, chirping of a robin.

"I must be careful," Nancy thought. "I'd be foolish to try tracking the thief alone. But if I don't follow him, I may lose a valuable clue."

As she pondered, her thoughts were jarred by the screech of brakes, accompanied by the skidding of tires on pavement.

Nancy's heart skipped a beat. A sickening thought flashed through her mind. Maybe someone was coming to meet the man in the woods!

"I may be trapped!" she chided herself. "What a goose I was to walk right into it!"

She hastened toward the road, carefully concealing herself from the newcomer. When Nancy saw the other car she gave a sigh of relief. In it were Bess and another girl, with the boyish name of George Fayne.

"Hi!" George called gaily. "What's the idea of going sleuthing without us?"

George, as well as Bess, had shared many of Nancy's exciting adventures. George, athletic and outspoken, was a striking contrast to her mild-mannered cousin Bess.

Nancy did not answer her dark-haired friend. She motioned for the two girls to get out of the car quickly and follow her.

"I think I'm on the trail of the person who stole the vase," she explained, starting off.

Bess locked her car and followed the others. Footprints were clearly visible in the woods. But fifty feet farther on they vanished in the thick undergrowth. There was no sign of the man.

"Oh dear!" Nancy said, disappointed.

George grinned. "What did you expect—that he was going to wait for you?"

Reluctantly Nancy turned back. "I know one thing about the man who was here," she said, "whether he's the vase thief or not. He's not very tall."

"How do you know?" Bess asked.

"By the small footprint and the short stride. Also, he wears lifts in his shoes," Nancy replied.

"Hypers!" said George, using one of her pet expressions. "You slay me!"

"Tell me about the shoes," Bess demanded.

Nancy explained. "These imprints are deeper than the usual footprints, and here's the trademark, anyway." She pointed to the heelprint. "I just happened to read an ad yesterday about this make of elevator shoes."

"Nancy, what are you up to?" asked George. "Bess told me about the stolen vase and elephant. Is that why you came here?"

"Not exactly. I was on my way to Masonville to look for a leaning chimney."

"A what?" George demanded.

Nancy explained about the clue to the China clay pit, and that it might be in Masonville.

"That's where we're going," said Bess. "To that darling dress shop next to the inn. How about having lunch with us?"

"Love to," Nancy replied. "Meet you at the inn at one o'clock."

Bess and George hopped into their car and followed Nancy. Entering the outskirts of Masonville, Nancy slowed her car and motioned she would leave the girls and start her sleuthing.

She drove around the city slowly in ever-narrowing circles, her keen eyes alert for a chimney that leaned, bent, curved, or was anything but perpendicular. At the end of half an hour, she was convinced she had never seen so many smokestacks in her life.

Then suddenly she saw it. A chimney that clearly leaned at an angle of several degrees!

"This is luck!" she told herself elatedly.

The chimney was on a house next to the corner dwelling in a row of old-fashioned, red-brick homes. The chimney was the only feature that distinguished the house from the others. The adjoining corner house was boarded up.

Nancy parked the car at the curb in front of the house with the leaning chimney. As she climbed the creaking steps to the porch and rang the bell, she saw a sign in the front window: ROOMS FOR RENT.

After a short interval, a white-haired, elderly woman came to the door, wiping her hands on an apron. She adjusted her spectacles and looked at Nancy inquiringly. The young detective smiled and said a trifle self-consciously:

"I know this sounds a little silly, but I've been looking for a leaning chimney and the first one I've found is yours. I've been told the chimney may have some connection with China clay."

The woman looked puzzled. "China clay?" she repeated slowly. "What do you mean?"

"Perhaps I'd better introduce myself," said Nancy. "My name is Nancy Drew—"

"Nancy Drew!" the woman interposed with surprise. "From River Heights?" When Nancy nodded, she added, "Is Mrs. Gruen your housekeeper?"

It was Nancy's turn to show surprise. "Yes, do you know Hannah?"

The white-haired old lady chuckled. "Land sakes, yes! I helped Hannah's mother take care of her when she was a little girl." She opened the door wider and stepped aside. "Come in and sit for a while. I'm Mrs. Wendell."

"Oh, I've heard Hannah speak of you." Nancy smiled. "I've wanted to meet you."

Nancy went into the neat, old-fashioned living room and sat down. Hastily removing her apron, Mrs. Wendell settled herself in a rocker.

"How is Hannah? I haven't seen her in so long."

"Oh, she's fine," Nancy answered politely. Then she steered the conversation back to China clay.

Mrs. Wendell was thoughtful for a moment, then she said:

"I've been living in this house for several years, Nancy, and never saw nor heard of a pit of China clay anywhere in the neighborhood. But—now let me see," she added, moving gently back and forth in the rocker. "I have something that may help you.

"There's an old trunk in the attic room. It belonged to Mr. Petersen, who sold me the house. He's dead now. The trunk's got some old papers and maps in it. I've been hankering to read them, but somehow never got around to it. Getting old, I guess. No curiosity left."

Nancy laughed.

"Seems to me if the leaning chimney's got anything to do with the China clay you're looking for," continued Mrs. Wendell, "the papers might mention it."

Nancy listened with mounting interest. "I'd like to look at them," she told Mrs. Wendell.

"All right," the woman agreed. "I'll fetch my keys."

She went to the kitchen, then returned and they started slowly up the long, narrow stairs. Arriving at the third floor, Mrs. Wendell knocked gently on a door.

"I'm sure Mr. Manning, who rents this room, isn't home," she said. "He hardly ever is around during the day."

When there was no answer, she turned a key in the lock. Just then the front doorbell rang.

"Seems every time I come upstairs the bell rings!" Mrs. Wendell sighed. "You go along inside. The trunk is in the closet."

Nancy entered the small, one-windowed room. It was simply furnished with an iron bedstead, a chest of drawers, and two straight-backed chairs. A washbasin sat on a wooden stand under a mirror next to a closet door. She walked across the room and opened the door.

"Oh!" Nancy gasped.

A man was just stepping through a panel in the rear of the closet!

Quick as a flash he stepped back. The panel slid across the space and a lock clicked into place.

"Mrs. Wendell! Come here!" Nancy cried at the top of her lungs.

Nancy quickly thrust aside a couple of suits that dangled on a rack and tried to open the panel. It would not budge. She examined the faint cracks in the closet wall that outlined the panel. They might easily go unnoticed in the subdued light. Then she turned to see the startled landlady.

"A man just sneaked through a panel in the back of this closet," said Nancy.

"Well, I never—!" Mrs. Wendell exclaimed in astonishment, then she began to tremble nervously.

Nancy dashed to the window and looked out to see if anyone would leave the adjoining vacant building. Glimpsing no one, she raced downstairs and looked on the street. The intruder did not appear.

"He must be hiding back of the panel," Nancy decided, and reported this to Mrs. Wendell. "Shall we break through?"

"If you think we should," the woman said shakily. "There's a hatchet in the basement."

Nancy got it and returned to the attic.

"Stand back, Mrs. Wendell," she warned, raising the hatchet.

Nancy gave the secret panel several hard whacks. The partition sagged. Then a final bang sent it flying into the space beyond.

She stepped through the narrow opening. After a second's hesitation, Mrs. Wendell followed. They stood in the attic of the corner house. The room was empty. Whoever had closed the secret panel had disappeared!

Nancy went to the door. It was locked, but the key was on the inside. Apparently the thief had not gone out that way.

She investigated a closet, Mrs. Wendell holding her breath in fear. No one was inside the cobwebby space.

Puzzled as to where the man had gone, Nancy noticed that the room's single, dirty window was half open. Lifting it all the way, she looked out just in time to see a man's hand grip the top of the high back-yard fence, then disappear!

Pursuit, Nancy figured, would be useless. The man had too much of a head start.

"We'd better call the police," she suggested.

"Oh dear!" said Mrs. Wendell. "I never thought I'd get mixed up with the police."

"I wonder how he got down," Nancy mused. She leaned out the window. The answer to the riddle was apparent. A foot away was a rainspout, entwined with heavy vines. It would be a simple matter for someone to cling to the vines and climb down to the ground.

As Nancy turned around, Mrs. Wendell gave a loud sneeze. The sound echoed through the musty attic.

"Such dust!" she said. "Nancy, what do you make of all this?"

"I don't like it."

Glancing about the room, Nancy saw several packages on the floor. They were wrapped with newspapers and tied with string. She bent over one of them and examined it closely. The newspaper was printed in Chinese!

Quickly untying the string, Nancy opened the bundle. It contained a beautiful Chinese vase decorated with lotus blossoms!

She untied a second bundle, then a third. They, too, held exquisite Oriental vases.

Mrs. Wendell stared at the porcelains in amazement. "My lands!" she burst out. "Where did *they* come from?"

Nancy had a hunch about that. But she decided to say nothing of her suspicions for the present.

"Don't be worried," Nancy begged. "Everything will come out all right."

Mrs. Wendell went downstairs. She waited a moment for one of her roomers to leave, then called police headquarters.

Meanwhile, Nancy unwrapped the remainder of the bundles. Each one contained a beautiful Oriental vase. She had hoped Mr. Soong's Ming piece and the jade elephant would be among them, but she was disappointed.

The Chinese newspapers intrigued her. After

carefully unfolding one of them she stuck part of it in her handbag.

Two Masonville policemen arrived, and Mrs. Wendell at once told them of Nancy's prowess as a detective. Nancy smiled and explained what had happened.

"What was the fellow like?" asked one of the officers, named McCann.

Nancy said she regretted not having had a better look at the intruder so that she might identify him, but the man had his head down as he was stepping through the opening.

"Looks like you discovered something big, Miss Drew," said Officer McCann as he picked up the vase patterned with lotus blossoms.

"This one fits the description of a vase stolen from the Masonville Museum last week," Officer McCann declared. He turned to Mrs. Wendell. "What do you know about all this stuff, ma'am?"

Mrs. Wendell was flustered, but Nancy put her arm reassuringly around the woman's shoulder as she spoke up falteringly:

"I don't know anything about it, Officer."

"Who lives in this room?" he asked, stepping back into the attic room.

Mrs. Wendell told of having rented it to a John Manning six months before. He had asked to be left alone because he was working very hard "writing a book" and did not want to be disturbed. The secret panel mystified her, she said. She was sure it had not been there before Manning rented the room.

"Manning probably installed it while you and the other tenants were away from the house," Officer McCann declared. "What does he look like?"

"Why, he's medium tall," the woman reflected, "with black hair and sort of olive skin. He . . . he spoke very nice, not like a rough thief. Seemed to me like he'd traveled a great deal."

"Um." The officer pondered, as if mentally reviewing the rogues' gallery.

"Oh, and he has piercing black eyes," Mrs. Wendell added quickly.

At once Nancy recalled the piercing black eyes of the strange-acting man she and Bess had encountered the previous night. Her gaze wandered around the floor of the room and the closet. "Mrs. Wendell," she asked, "did you ever notice anything unusual about the height of Mr. Manning's shoes?"

"Why, no," she said, somewhat surprised.

Nancy told the policeman about the unusual footprints she had found at Hunter's Bridge. He agreed that the prints might well have been made by the thief, and that the thief might be the man known as John Manning.

While the three had been talking, the other policeman had been examining the attics in both houses, searching for additional loot. Finding none, he wrapped up several of Manning's personal belongings to study later for fingerprints and compare them with those on the vases. Finally the two officers gathered together the pieces of pottery and started down the stairs.

"If you ever want a job on the Masonville force, let us know!" one of them said to Nancy.

"I really only stumbled on this," Nancy said modestly. "I came here looking for a leaning chimney and found an attic full of loot."

The policemen glanced at each other incredulously. "A leaning chimney?" echoed McCann. "And that led you to discover a crook?"

The other officer cocked his head. "I guess that's what they call woman's intuition. I wish I had some of it!"

After the police officers had descended the stairs, accompanied by Mrs. Wendell, Nancy looked about Manning's room. What a sight! Dresser drawers were pulled out, the mattress overturned, the rug rolled back, the contents of the trunk scattered over the floor. Even the cardboard backing had been removed from the pictures. Manning's suits had been examined also. The pockets had been turned inside out and their linings inspected.

"I wonder if there could be anything the police missed," Nancy mused as she surveyed the room.

True, they had found plenty of loot, but they

had not uncovered a single thing that might be a clue to the identity of the thief.

"The floor!" Nancy said half-aloud. The police hadn't examined the floorboards.

Getting to her knees, the young detective scrutinized the rough-hewn planks. Perhaps a loose one might have served as a hiding place for Manning's mail. But every board was secured by big, broad nails used by carpenters sixty years before.

"Nothing there," sighed Nancy, rising to her feet.

Then a thought flashed through her mind. "The window shade!"

Nancy had a sudden vision of letters falling from the tightly rolled-up shade when she pulled it down. Going to the window, she tugged the cord. The shade came halfway down, but no letters fluttered to her feet.

Nancy made a discovery, however. The sun, streaming through the window, faintly outlined some dark squares on the shade. Excitedly Nancy removed the shade from its little brass fixtures and laid it on the bed.

"This *is* a find!" she mused in puzzled delight.

Taped to the outside of the shade were four pages torn from an art magazine. They were full-color photographs of rare old Chinese vases!

Attached slightly above them were two yellow sheets of paper listing the museums and homes where the vases could be found!

CHAPTER IV

The Blinding Glare

"THAT's pretty conclusive proof Manning's the thief," Nancy told herself. "I'll take these papers to the police."

It was easy to understand how they had overlooked the papers Manning had concealed so cunningly in the shade. She unrolled it another foot. More papers were attached. Each contained Chinese writing done in bold brush strokes with black ink.

"I wonder what they mean," Nancy thought. "They must have something to do with the vases."

Just then she glanced at her watch. Less than half an hour to meet Bess and George! She had not even looked through the contents of the old trunk for a clue to the China clay pit!

Carefully Nancy removed the papers from their hiding place and put them in her handbag. While she was restoring the shade to the window, Mrs.

Wendell returned. She said the police would send a man to watch the house, but they doubted that Manning would return.

"And I got a carpenter comin' right away to board up that hole into the other house," Mrs. Wendell reported.

Nancy told of her new find, then looked over the contents of the trunk. Scattered among old clothes were a lot of yellowed letters. Nancy scanned the correspondence. Much of it was personal, so she read only enough to convince herself there was no mention of China clay.

"Mrs. Wendell," she said, "did Mr. Manning ever say anything about this trunk?"

The woman looked startled. "Yes, he talked quite a bit about it. He said it wouldn't bother him in the room and insisted I leave it here. Why did you ask?"

"I believe he might have come here on purpose to look for something in it; something that belonged to Mr. Petersen."

"Oh, gracious!" said Mrs. Wendell. "This gets more complicated every minute."

"Don't worry any more about it." Nancy patted the woman's arm. "Just forget the whole thing."

Nancy said good-by and went to her car. She drove as rapidly as she dared in order to keep her date with Bess and George at the Masonville Inn. But when she reached it, she was minutes late.

"Well," said George when Nancy had parked, "I hope you don't keep Ned Nickerson waiting like this!"

Nancy blushed, thinking of Ned, a student at Emerson College. Nancy enjoyed his company, and had attended many parties and dances with him.

"I just couldn't get here any sooner," Nancy replied. "Wait till you hear about the secret panel!"

At lunch Nancy told her friends what had happened. Bess's eyes grew wide with astonishment and George said, "Gosh!" and "Hypers!" several times.

After Nancy had finished eating, she showed the girls the photographs of the vases, then copied the Chinese symbols in a notebook.

"We'd better go," said Bess. "I said I'd be home by four."

"Oh, heck!" George complained. "That dress I bought won't be ready for an hour." She explained that it was being altered slightly.

"I bought two dresses, Nancy," said Bess. "They're positively yummy."

"Um." Nancy smiled. Then, pretending to be envious, she said, "I'll be at Helen Townsend's birthday dinner tonight in just an old pink sheath. Tell you what. Suppose you go on home, Bess, and I'll wait for George. I want to stop at police headquarters with these papers."

The arrangement suited Bess, who drove off at once. She took a longer but more traveled road back to River Heights than the one where the suspected thief had been.

An hour later Nancy and George followed but took the short cut. Nancy braked as the convertible went around the series of twisting curves approaching Hunter's Bridge.

"Do you think the man you saw here was Manning?" George asked. She leaned forward, looking alertly ahead, as if she expected the man to jump out at them any moment.

"Either Manning or a pal," Nancy answered. "Mr. Soong's vase wasn't in that attic."

"But it would have reached there eventually if you hadn't spoiled Manning's plans," said George. "I wonder where Mr. Soong's vase is."

Nancy was about to reply when suddenly both girls were blinded by a stabbing glare. Nancy threw up her left hand to shield her eyes. Then, as quickly as the glare had come, it disappeared.

"What was that?" George asked.

Nancy stopped and got out. "I don't know," she said. "But I intend to find out."

"Not without me," George declared.

Together the girls walked to the sparse woods from which the flash had come. In a few seconds Nancy and George came upon a car. It was a maroon coupé with a badly dented right rear fender. The car was empty.

Attached to the outside frame was a side-view mirror. It had been tilted, possibly by the jarring trip off the road. On a hunch, Nancy adjusted the mirror. As she did so, she was struck by the same stabbing glare that had blinded her in the convertible. A ray of sunlight had been reflected from it to the road!

"Funny place to leave a car," George commented.

"This may be a meeting place for Manning and his friends." Nancy circled the coupe, then jotted down the license number in her notebook.

As if confirming her deduction, Nancy and George heard the murmur of men's voices deeper in the woods. The girls started forward.

Taking care not to make a sound, they stepped cautiously as the voices grew more distinct. Presently the girls saw two men. Their backs were turned, and they seemed to be bending over something on a log. Unable to hear what they were saying, Nancy and George crept forward.

Nancy's attention was so fixed on the men that she did not notice a dry twig in her path. The next moment, there was a sharp crack as she stepped on the twig.

The girls heard a startled exclamation, followed by a hollow crash, as if something had dropped and broken. Without looking back, the men scooted into the brush and disappeared.

"George, I'll see what they dropped," Nancy

whispered, running quickly toward the log.

"Be right back!" called George, and raced off in the direction of the disappearing men.

Hoping that they would be heading for their car, George plunged into the dense underbrush. She had to get a look at them!

Beside the log, Nancy found part of a wrinkled newspaper. On it lay fragments of what had been a small Oriental bowl. Nancy glanced at the newspaper. It was Chinese!

She bent over to pick up the paper and the broken pieces. They might prove to be a valuable clue. But hardly had she put the last fragment in her bag when a bloodcurdling scream rent the woods.

It came from George!

Nancy raced pell-mell toward the sound, which had come from the direction of the car. Her worst fears aroused, she fairly flew, heedless of the brambles that tore at her dress. Finally she came in sight of the coupé standing exactly where she had seen it.

George was not there!

As Nancy stood uncertain under a low-hanging limb, a shadowy figure suddenly leaped at her. She felt a stinging pain and collapsed to the ground!

CHAPTER V

A Chinese Puzzle

NANCY recovered her senses in a few minutes and got up. There was a dull throbbing in her forehead, but her memory cleared at once.

Her first thought was of George. There was no sign of her. The maroon coupé was gone, and for an instant Nancy was fearful her friend might have been kidnapped. But she discarded the horrible thought at once.

"More than likely George was knocked out too," she reasoned.

Picking up her handbag, which lay on the ground, she began calling George's name. To Nancy's relief, the shout was answered.

"I'm over here! Blindfolded! My hands are tied!"

Nancy traced the sound. George stood with her back to a tree, rubbing her wrists against the bark to tear off the belt of her dress with which they

41

were bound. Nancy quickly freed her and removed the blindfold. George's story differed only slightly from Nancy's.

"It all happened so fast!" George said. She took a deep breath. "I thought I'd lost the men. When I turned around to go back to you, one of them jumped out of the bushes and tied my scarf over my eyes. I screamed and tried to tear it off. But another man bound my hands and told me to keep still!"

"Did you see either of them?" Nancy asked.

"Not enough of their faces to identify them."

Nancy led the way out of the woods to the road. The girls, disappointed and chagrined, but thankful nothing harmful had happened, climbed into Nancy's car and headed for home.

Suddenly George shook off the mood and grinned. "Those fellows were pretty dumb," she said. "You have their license number."

"And they left some other evidence." Nancy told of the pieces of the bowl still in her purse. "One of the men might have been Manning."

Some time later Nancy stopped in front of George's house, and her friend got out. "See you tonight at Helen's birthday party."

"You bet. I wouldn't miss it for anything!"

Nancy drove to the motor-vehicle office to learn the name of the owner of the maroon coupé, if possible. The man in charge knew her, and after hearing her story, obligingly telephoned state headquarters for the information.

"You just got here in time," he said, while holding the telephone. "We're about to close."

He found that the license plates had been issued to a Paul Scott of Masonville, and that the coupe had been reported stolen that very afternoon!

"I'll bet those men planned to hide the car in the woods until they could paint it another color and put different license plates on it," Nancy said to the man. "May I call the police?"

"Sure thing. Use my desk phone."

After Nancy had talked to Police Chief McGinnis, she drove to Dick Milton's shop and told him about the leaning chimney in Masonville. Dick was disappointed that the clue had not led to a China clay pit. Then Nancy left him and headed for Mr. Drew's office. She had promised to pick up her father at six o'clock.

Fortunately an automobile pulled away from the curb in front of the building where Carson Drew had his law office. Nancy skillfully guided the convertible into the vacant spot. As she was about to get out, she saw a short Chinese gentleman with spectacles and a tiny goatee emerge from the building.

"Mr. Soong!" she called.

The Chinese smiled and came over to her.

"You're just the person I want to see!" Nancy greeted him. "Can you spare a minute?"

Mr. Soong nodded. He looked very natty in a gray felt hat and a blue pin-striped suit. He carried a handsome Malacca cane. Nancy opened the door and he seated himself beside her.

"May I drive you home?" she asked.

"That would be very kind. I must hurry to keep an engagement."

On the way, she told Mr. Soong of her day's adventures. The Oriental gentleman's face reflected his amazement. He could not identify John Manning, but he begged Nancy to be extremely careful in further investigations.

When Nancy pulled up at Mr. Soong's home, she opened her bag and took out the wrinkled newspaper which held the broken fragments of a Chinese bowl. But first she showed Mr. Soong the symbols she had copied.

"I hope they're not as mystifying to you as they are to me," Nancy remarked.

It is no mystery what they mean," he replied.

He translated the first set of symbols on the sheet, pointing his finger at each character as he spoke. "Made in the studio of deep peace."

Nancy looked at him, perplexed, but he went on to the second group of characters. "Made for the hall of fragrant virtue," he translated.

Mr. Soong smiled at Nancy's puzzled expression. "Each set of symbols is a sort of Chinese

"It is no mystery what the symbols mean,"
Mr. Soong replied

hallmark," he explained. "That is to say, they're like the little mark an American manufacturer sometimes stamps on his products."

"I know what you mean," Nancy interposed. "I've seen such marks on silver and gold."

Mr. Soong nodded in quick agreement. "Such symbols have been used for centuries by the Chinese to designate an article as authentic and of fine workmanship," he said. "They go back centuries to the great Sung, Ming, and Ch'in dynasties."

"How interesting!" said Nancy.

Mr. Soong peered again at the symbols. "These particular sets of markings are very old and famous," he said. "They are from the Ming dynasty and are well known to all experts on porcelains."

"Oh!" exclaimed Nancy. "I'm learning more than I had hoped!" Her brow knit in a frown. "But what use would Manning have for copies of the markings?" she persisted. "And why should he take such pains to conceal them?"

Mr. Soong gave a gentle shrug and smiled. "That I do not know."

Nancy showed him the Chinese newspaper she had taken from the attic in Masonville. It was a Chinese daily published in New York, Mr. Soong told her.

"This Mr. Manning may work with Chinese in New York," he suggested.

Next, Nancy opened the wrinkled newspaper

which held the fragments of the broken bowl. The paper, Nancy saw, was the same as the other.

Mr. Soong examined the pieces with interest, but they were so small he could tell only that the bowl had been made of excellent clay. He looked at Nancy inquiringly, as if to ask for more information. But she shook her head with a sigh.

"They're all the leads I have—this time!" she replied.

Mr. Soong stepped from the car and gravely shook Nancy's hand.

"You have done very well, Miss Drew," he said softly. "With the help of both members of your illustrious family, I am confident that my unworthy problems will soon be solved."

The Chinese bowed slightly, then turned and went up the walk to his front door. Nancy looked after him, puzzled. "Now, what did he mean by that?" she asked herself.

Nancy hurried back to her father's office building. While she was trying to squeeze into a parking space, a familiar voice said:

"Mind if I take you home?"

Nancy looked around swiftly. "Dad!" she cried.

She planted a kiss on his cheek as he got in. Carson Drew was a tall, handsome man of middle age, with alert blue eyes like those of his daughter. Like Nancy's, too, they twinkled when his sense of humor was aroused.

The relationship between Nancy and her father

was warm and companionable. No matter how busy Mr. Drew was with his own criminal cases, he always found time to discuss Nancy's cases.

Now, driving home, the distinguished-looking attorney and his attractive daughter talked about her latest adventures. As Nancy swung the convertible into the driveway of the Drew home, she suddenly remembered Mr. Soong's parting words. Nancy repeated them to her father and asked if he knew what they meant.

"You bet I do. Mr. Soong paid me a visit today. He wants you and me to undertake a search."

"A search?"

"That's right. A Chinese puzzle that goes back five years!"

He got out of the car and Nancy quickly followed him.

"Dad, stop keeping me in suspense!" she begged. "What's it all about?"

"I'll tell when we get inside," he promised, mounting the steps to the porch. "It's the story of the missing Engs!"

CHAPTER VI

The Vanishing Vase

"WHAT are the missing Engs?" Nancy inquired when she and her father were seated in his study. "Some valuable jewels?"

Mr. Drew laughed. "You're not even warm! The Engs are Chinese friends of Mr. Soong's; Eng Moy and his daughter Eng Lei. As you know," he added, "Chinese last names come first!"

Carson Drew paused for a moment.

"Go on, Dad," Nancy begged impatiently.

"Five years ago Eng Moy wrote to Mr. Soong from China. He said he and his daughter were leaving on a trip to the United States and hoped to visit him. According to Mr. Soong, Eng Moy was a well-known maker of porcelains in China. The purpose of his trip was to study American pottery methods."

"Did Eng Lei make pottery, too?" Nancy asked.

Her father shook his head. "Not at the time

49

the Engs left China, at any rate. She was only twelve years old then. That means she's about seventeen now."

"When did they disappear?" Nancy asked, interested at once in hearing about a girl so close to her own age.

"That's coming. Eng Moy continued to write to Mr. Soong," Mr. Drew explained. "Eng described tours they had taken through pottery plants in several cities in the United States. Each succeeding letter was postmarked a little closer to River Heights. Finally Mr. Soong received a letter saying they would visit him the following week."

The lawyer paused.

"And they didn't come?" Nancy asked.

"No. That was four and a half years ago. Mr. Soong hasn't heard from the Engs since!"

"Maybe something happened so they couldn't write."

"That's what Mr. Soong would like to find out," Mr. Drew replied. "He came to my office today because he had received a letter from a relative in China. Mr. Soong supposed the Engs had returned to the Orient without paying him the promised visit. He had been a bit perplexed when his letters to China were never acknowledged."

"Sounds very strange," said Nancy.

"He learned something from the letter he received today," said Mr. Drew. "The relative wrote that the Engs never had returned to China and the United States immigration authorities could not account for it."

"Then the Engs are probably still in this country," Nancy reasoned.

"Seems that way," her father agreed. "Mr. Soong fears his friends have met with—well, let's call it foul play."

"What do *you* suspect happened to them?" Nancy asked.

"I don't suspect anything yet," Mr. Drew replied. "But there are several reasons why some aliens want United States authorities to lose track of them. Espionage is one. Receiving and selling smuggled goods is another."

"Not a friend of Mr. Soong's!" said Nancy, shocked.

Her father smiled dryly, "You're probably right, but that doesn't solve the mystery."

Nancy looked at her father searchingly, then asked how she might help on the case.

Mr. Drew smiled affectionately. "As soon as I get a clue, I'll put you to work on it."

"Thanks, Dad." Nancy looked at her watch and gave a start. "My goodness, I must run or I'll be late for Helen's birthday dinner!"

She dashed upstairs to dress. A few minutes later Nancy hurried down, blew a kiss to her father, and waved good-by to Mrs. Gruen.

"Wait a moment," the housekeeper said. "You

worry me, Nancy," she said. "It will be late when you leave the Townsend house and I don't like your coming home alone."

"I'll soon settle this," Mr. Drew declared. "Hannah, I'll drive my daughter and her friends to Helen's and go back for them."

Twenty minutes later he dropped Bess, George, and Nancy across town. Mr. Townsend teased the girls with a "Glad you made it. I'd begun to think I'd have to eat four pieces of birthday cake!"

Helen smiled and said, "If I know Nancy, she probably was tracking down some villain."

"That's right." Nancy laughed. "A new way to say 'Happy Birthday.'"

Helen took the girls' coats and handbags upstairs to her room.

In a few minutes Mrs. Townsend called everyone into the dining room. As Nancy was about to follow, she noticed an exquisite vase on the desk near a window. She lifted the vase carefully and examined the porcelain.

It was in a lovely shade of brown, showing a peach tree at the edge of a sparkling blue lake. An ancient Chinese, attired in a richly brocaded robe, sat under the tree beside a deer.

Nancy studied the bottom of the base. Painted with small, black brush strokes were several Chinese symbols. They seemed to be the same as one set of characters she had copied from the sheets in Manning's room!

Nancy ran upstairs and got her clutch bag. Then, seating herself at the living-room desk, she took a pen from its ornate holder and quickly copied the symbols. She dried the ink on a small blotter which lay on the desk and slipped the paper into her bag.

She was about to go into the dining room when she spotted two strange marks cunningly worked into the leaves of the peach tree. Nancy stared at the small, barely visible markings. The more she looked the more puzzled she became. Before she could copy the little symbols, Mrs. Townsend hurried into the room.

"Nancy, come on!" she coaxed.

"I'm sorry," Nancy apologized. "This vase—"

"Like it?" Helen's mother asked.

"Love it!" Nancy replied. "It's one of the finest I've ever seen."

"It's a Ming vase. My husband gave it to me for an anniversary present," Mrs. Townsend said, leading the way into the dining room.

Nancy followed. As she ate, the young detective kept thinking about what she had just discovered. After the birthday cake had been served, Helen began to unwrap her gifts. "Ohs" and "Ahs" greeted each gaily wrapped package. Besides several pieces of beautiful lingerie, she received an attractive figurine Bess had made in Dick Milton's pottery class.

"Oh, it's lovely!" she exclaimed. "Thanks heaps, Bess."

There was a roar of laughter as a baseball glove from George was opened. But this was something Helen had said she wanted, months before, and no one would give it to her!

Nancy's gift was the surprise of the evening. She had prearranged with Mrs. Townsend that it would be brought in last. Cuddled on a cushion in a little pink basket was a fluffy white kitten.

"Nancy, you darling!" Helen burst out. "You remembered I've been meaning to get one."

The girls gathered around to admire the kitten. Then, as the hands of the clock moved toward ten-thirty, the guests said they must leave.

Nancy, Bess, and George went upstairs for their coats. When Nancy came down carrying her coat, she went to the desk to get her bag. She stopped short in surprise. The bag was gone!

When Mrs. Townsend and the others came downstairs Nancy asked them if they had seen her bag. But none of them knew anything about it.

"What could have become of it?" Mr. Townsend asked, joining the search.

Nancy noticed that the window near the desk was partly open. Could someone have reached in and taken the bag?

"May I have a flashlight?" she asked.

Obtaining one from Mr. Townsend, she dashed

out the front door and went around to the side of the house, followed by the others. Under the partly opened window was a flower bed. In it were footprints!

At that moment she heard Mrs. Townsend call, "Isn't this yours, Nancy?"

Nancy turned. Helen's mother was holding out the familiar blue bag.

"Yes, that's mine," Nancy said. "Thank you. Where did you find it?"

"It was lying here in the grass," Mrs. Townsend explained.

"Oh, I hope nothing's gone," said Helen.

Nancy opened the bag, feeling sure all the contents would be missing. At first glance it seemed as if only the money in it was gone. Then she realized that the paper on which she had copied the Chinese symbols from the vase was also missing.

Suddenly Nancy was struck by a dismaying thought. Without a word, she darted into the house. Her worst fears were confirmed.

The Townsends' beautiful, rare vase had vanished!

CHAPTER VII

Three on a Clue

NANCY stared in dismay at the vacant spot on the desk. Then she ran into the kitchen, snapped on the back-yard light, and dashed outside. Nobody was there.

By then Mr. and Mrs. Townsend and the girls had caught up to her. "What's the matter now, Nancy?" asked Mr. Townsend.

As she told them about the stolen vase, Nancy experienced a sudden twinge of guilt. If the thief had not observed her copying the symbols on the bottom, he might never have stolen the vase. But why was her copy of the symbols so important to him?

Suddenly Nancy thought she knew. She ran to the side of the house, fully expecting to see the same identifying footprints she had spotted at Hunter's Bridge; prints she believed were Manning's. But she was disappointed. These marks were short and wide.

When she told Bess and George the idea she had had about the footprints, George was inclined to think the thief was some pal of Manning's.

"He's probably one of those men in the woods," she added.

"And has been told to trail you, Nancy," Bess said fearfully.

"Hypers!" said George. "This puts such a damper on everything."

The other girls murmured in agreement. The Townsends insisted upon hearing about the case. Nancy told what she deemed necessary, then Mr. Townsend went to telephone the police. Two officers arrived, made a routine check indoors and out, then queried Nancy.

After they had gone, a thought suddenly flashed through Nancy's mind. She went to the desk and picked up the small blotter she had used to dry the ink on her notation of the Chinese characters. They were clearly reproduced in reverse.

"I'll take this home and compare the symbols with those on the paper there," she decided.

Nancy slipped the blotter into her bag and turned back to speak to Mr. Townsend. "Where did you buy the vase?"

"Why, let me see," he replied, reaching into his inside coat pocket. "I think I have the name of the shop right here in my wallet. Yes, here it is. Sen-yung's Oriental Gift Shop, Madison Avenue, New York."

Nancy made a mental note of the name.

Mr. Drew arrived shortly to take the girls home. Upon hearing of the theft, and the possibility that Nancy had been spied upon, he was glad he had escorted the girls to the party and back. Nancy, Bess, and George thanked their hostess for the lovely party, then left.

When the Drews reached home, they sat down for a few minutes to discuss the strange turn of events. Nancy took the blotter from her bag and handed it to her father. Then she went to her room to get a hand mirror and the sheet of paper containing the Chinese symbols found in Manning's room. Holding the blotter up to the mirror, she saw at a glance that the writing was the same as one set of characters on the sheet. It read:

"Made for the hall of fragrant virtue."

Nancy was thrilled at the new clue. But she was still puzzled over the thief's motive for stealing her copy of the symbols.

In the morning Nancy telephoned the Townsends to say again how lovely the birthday party had been, and to ask if there was any news of the thief.

"Not a speck," Helen replied. "Say, Nancy, maybe you could find the thief for us."

"If I get any clues, I'll let you know," Nancy promised, and hung up.

Since she could think of no way at the moment to trace the thief, Nancy decided to concentrate on finding the China clay pit. She went to the River Heights Public Library to scan books on local geology. But after poring over several volumes and maps, Nancy had found nothing.

She closed the books with a sigh and put them back on the shelf. Miss Carter, the librarian, had noticed Nancy's disappointed expression.

"Couldn't you find what you're looking for?" she inquired pleasantly.

Nancy shook her head and told the librarian the nature of her quest.

"Why don't you ask Miles Monroe?" Miss Carter suggested. "He's a retired professor of geology. If anyone knows of a clay deposit, he should. I'll give you his address."

"Thank you," Nancy said, smiling. "I'll go to see him at once."

The geologist lived in a small apartment. She pushed the buzzer under Miles Monroe's name card and in a moment a small peephole flew open. An eye stared at Nancy.

"If you're selling something," boomed a voice, "I don't want any of it!"

Nancy stifled a laugh. "I'm not a saleswoman. I came to see you about a geology problem!"

The eye stared a moment longer. Then the peephole snapped shut and the door flew open. A man stood in the doorway, looking Nancy up and down. He was tall and slightly stoop-shouldered, with a sharp, inquisitive face and a thatch of bristling red hair.

"Geology problem!" he snorted. "You're too pretty for such heavy thoughts. But come in!"

As Nancy followed the professor into the living room she noticed that he walked with a limp.

"Have a chair!" he said. Mr. Monroe seated himself, looking straight at Nancy. "Well, young lady," he asked, "what's on your mind?"

After Nancy introduced herself, she told of her search for a deposit of China clay. Monroe said he knew of none in the state.

"I've heard," Nancy went on, "that it may be identified in some way with a leaning chimney."

Miles Monroe scoffed. "First time I ever heard of using a chimney to find a vein of kaolin!"

"Kaolin?" repeated Nancy.

The professor replied, "That's what geologists call the fine white clay used in the manufacture of china and porcelain. The name comes from the Chinese *Kaoling*. It's a mountain in China which yielded the first kaolin."

Nancy eagerly absorbed this new knowledge as Miles Monroe added:

"Kaolin is formed by the weathering of granite

and other rocks. Then the clay is washed free of the quartz and mixed with feldspar, flint, and so forth to make porcelain." He smiled wryly. "You may as well know what it's all about if you're looking for the stuff."

"Of course," Nancy agreed. "But I had hoped you'd be able to tell me about a pit of China clay in this region. It's supposed to be near Masonville."

Professor Monroe rubbed his nose. "Don't know much about the land around Masonville," he replied. "Had to give up my field trips when I injured my leg in a fall six years ago. That's when I retired. Before that, I lived in Philadelphia."

"Well, I'm sorry to have bothered you," Nancy said, rising.

"Say, wait a minute!" Miles Monroe burst out suddenly. "There's one section I had an interest in and was always going to get to. It's a stretch of woods several miles out of River Heights toward Masonville."

He gave her directions for reaching it.

"There's an abandoned Civil War iron mine and smelter out there, I was told. It may have a leaning chimney. If you find a China clay pit, I would like to know about it."

Nancy thanked him for the information. She was glad to have the lead, slim as it was.

Professor Monroe walked to the door with her,

and she went down to her car. Then she drove to George's home.

Her friend was mowing the front lawn. Seated on the ground was Bess, clipping a hedge.

Nancy tooted her horn. The two girls looked up and ran to the car.

"I'm going for a short drive in the country. Just got a new lead on the leaning chimney," Nancy told them. "Want to come along?"

Bess eyed her friend suspiciously. "What do we have to do?" she asked.

"What difference does it make as long as it's fun!" scoffed George. She slid into the seat beside Nancy.

"Okay. I'll go tell your mother where we're going, George."

Bess returned in a moment and hopped into the convertible. Nancy headed for Three Bridges Road.

"Oh, my goodness!" Bess exclaimed as they neared Hunter's Bridge. "This awful place again!"

"But this time we're not stopping," Nancy reassured her, and Bess sighed in relief.

Shortly after crossing Hunter's Bridge they came to a narrow gravel road which veered to the right. Nancy turned the car onto it.

After traveling about eight miles from River Heights, she pulled up under a tree and stopped. The three girls got out and started through the woods to search for the abandoned mine.

They walked for nearly an hour among trees and through stony pastures, climbing old, rotted fences and slapping at insects. Bess's enthusiasm began to wane.

"I'm tired," she moaned. "Let's go back. I'll bet Professor Monroe doesn't know what he's talking about."

Even George and Nancy wondered whether the old mine really existed.

"Just a little farther," Nancy urged.

"We'll be in the next state," joked George. "But I'm willing."

The three trudged on, when suddenly a barrier loomed up ahead. It was a high, board fence, topped by strands of rusty barbed wire. The three girls stopped and stared in amazement.

"Why would anyone put up such a thing in this wilderness?" Bess asked.

The girls inspected the fence closely. It was about ten feet high. The boards adjoined one another so snugly that only the narrowest of cracks appeared between them. Nancy tried to peer through one to see what lay on the other side, but she could make out nothing.

"Hypers!" exclaimed George. "The fence must be five hundred feet long!"

"Come on," Nancy urged. "Let's try to find an opening we can see through."

The girls walked along the fence, their eyes probing for a gate or a wide crack.

"Here's the end of the fence," announced Nancy, who was in the lead.

Indeed, it looked like the end, but it was only the end of one side. The board barrier turned sharply at a right angle and continued another two hundred and fifty feet.

When the girls arrived at the middle of the second stretch of fence, Nancy's alert eyes spotted a small knothole.

"At last!" she exclaimed.

Stepping up eagerly, she closed one eye and peeked through the hole with the other. At first she was unable to see much because of a growth of trees and bushes. Then, shifting her gaze, Nancy saw an old, battered brick wall running parallel to the fence, a short distance back from it. The wall was about eight feet high and was topped by a sloping roof. Obviously it was part of a building. But within the range of her vision Nancy could see no windows.

"Find anything?" George asked impatiently.

"Only an old—" Nancy stopped speaking as she caught sight of something jutting from the roof of the building. Then she cried excitedly:

"Girls, it's a leaning chimney!"

CHAPTER VIII

Mystery in Manhattan

"LET me see!" George exclaimed excitedly.

Nancy stepped aside so the dark-haired girl could look through the knothole.

"Maybe it's the abandoned iron mine and smelter!" put in Bess.

"There are so many trees, it's hard to see just what's inside," George said.

"If this is *the* leaning chimney we're looking for," Nancy reasoned, "the China clay pit must be somewhere nearby. Possibly inside the fence."

"Let's go," she suggested, starting along the enclosure. "There *must* be an opening somewhere."

"You lose," retorted George as the trio rounded the edge of the fence.

No opening was in sight. Instead, the unbroken expanse of boards extended another five hundred feet.

When the girls reached the end of this, the

fence took another right angle turn. This time it stretched two hundred and fifty feet.

Bess groaned. "Oh, I'm so tired—and hungry."

"Perhaps," teased George, "there's a baseball park inside. If there is, we'll stop at the frankfurter stand."

"Think we'll need a helicopter to get inside," Nancy joked, examining the boards closely. "These planks are certainly fitted tight together."

As they walked on, she kept turning over in her mind several things that mystified her: the air of secrecy about the enclosure, the seeming lack of doors, and the apparent lack of activity.

"Since we can't get in," Nancy said, "I'm going to try looking inside to see if I can spot any clay pit."

Making her way to a nearby tree, she shinned up to the first branch, then swung herself into the crotch of the tree.

"Find anything?" George asked.

"I can't see much better from here," Nancy reported. "Too many trees inside."

Suddenly she was struck by something near the top of the leaning chimney. It was a rusted iron ornament fastened to the bricks.

"What does it look like?" asked George when Nancy reported her discovery.

"A lot of crisscross bars," Nancy replied. "Maybe the coat of arms of the old mine owner."

As she climbed down, Bess called from a distance, where she was standing on a little knoll. "I've got a good view of it from here."

George started for the spot when suddenly Bess let out a terrifying scream. Her two friends ran toward her. When they reached the knoll, Bess was trembling with fear.

"What happened?" Nancy demanded.

"Oh, N-Nancy," Bess said, pointing, "I saw a bony hand reach out of the chimney!"

Nancy and George looked. There was no sign of a hand. Bess said she had closed her eyes a moment to shut out the weird sight. When she had opened them again, the hand was gone.

"I think you're goofy," George scoffed. "A person sees things when he gets tired."

"I'm not that tired," Bess retorted. "I saw it. I know I did."

In panic she dashed through the woods toward Nancy's car. There was nothing for the other girls to do but follow her.

Nancy started the motor. Soon they were a good distance from the eerie spot.

"I never want to go there again," Bess declared.

"Not even to help your cousin Dick?" Nancy asked with a grin.

Bess finally conceded maybe she would get over her fright, and she did want Dick to acquire the special clay if possible.

After Nancy drove the girls to their homes, she decided to drop into Dick's shop and tell him of her latest discovery. She found a high school boy, who clerked for the young pottery maker after school, behind the counter.

"Would you like something, miss?" he asked.

"I'd like to see Mr. Milton."

"He's busy in the back of the shop right now," the boy answered. "But he'll be through in a minute. Will you wait?"

Nancy smiled. "He's a friend of mine," she said. "I'll go back and see him."

In the rear room Dick was engrossed at the potter's wheel, his sandy hair tumbling over his forehead. He was so busy he did not notice his caller.

Nancy watched while Dick deftly pressed a lump of clay on the center of the wheel, then allowed it to rise between his fingers in a spiral column before depressing it.

Once more the column spiraled. The young man again pushed it down, at the same time centering and truing the clay. Then he pressed his thumbs into the soft clay, rapidly forming a cylinder.

With one hand inside the cylinder and the other outside, Dick molded the clay into the thickness he desired. Nancy now saw the cylinder shape like magic into a large jar.

Dick snapped off a switch and the whirring wheel slowly stopped. As he turned around, a look of pleased surprise spread over his face.

"Nancy Drew! How did you get here?"

"Simple. That jar you just made is Aladdin's lamp. You rubbed it . . . and I appeared!"

Dick laughed, then grew sober. "I wish we could conjure up a genie to find that China clay pit," he said a bit ruefully.

"Maybe we don't need a genie," said Nancy.

"What do you mean?"

"We may have found the leaning chimney!" Nancy beamed.

Dick gasped. "Honestly?"

"I don't know yet." Nancy told Dick what she and her friends had discovered. "I'm going back soon to look more thoroughly."

A boyish smile of hope lit Dick's face as he escorted Nancy to the door.

"I'll keep you posted on further developments," Nancy promised.

After dinner that evening she accompanied her father to his study on the second floor.

"You're up to something, young lady," he said shrewdly. "What is it?"

Nancy told him of her visit to the strange enclosure. Mr. Drew frowned.

"I don't like the sound of it," he said. "Strikes me as a good place to stay away from."

"But, Dad!" Nancy protested, her blue eyes growing large with emphasis. "There may be a valuable pit of China clay around there. And if I don't go back, I'll never find out!"

"If it's inside the fence, the owner probably won't want to sell the clay, anyway," Mr. Drew reminded his daughter. "Well, look around if you wish. But be careful. Don't go there alone."

"All right," she promised.

Carson Drew took a paper from his pocket and said, "I have a clue, too. It's about the Engs."

"What is it?" Nancy asked eagerly.

"I received a phone call from San Francisco this afternoon," Mr. Drew explained, "and my secretary wrote down this report." He settled back in his chair and continued:

"It says that when the Engs arrived in San Francisco, on their trip to the United States, they were met at the dock by a man named David Carr.

"Carr was sales representative for the West Coast Trading Company, a San Francisco importing house," Mr. Drew went on. "He and Eng Moy apparently were acquainted as the result of business dealings. When the Engs left San Francisco on their tour of United States pottery plants, Carr went with them."

"Does the report mention what David Carr looks like?" Nancy asked.

"No. The report says there doesn't appear to be any photograph or description of him available. Even the officials of the importing company can't furnish any clues. It seems that Carr did practically all his work for them in China; contacted

them by mail. Then, about the time he met the
Engs in San Francisco, he dropped out of sight."

"Maybe Carr has something to do with the
Engs' disappearance," Nancy speculated.

"Could be," her father agreed. He put the report away. "Anyway, it's a clue to work on."

As Nancy pondered, she glanced idly at a New
York City newspaper which lay on her father's
desk. Suddenly a small black headline caught her
eye. She picked up the paper and scanned the
story, then read it to her father.

It described a robbery that had taken place in
New York. An ancient Chinese tea jar, dating
from the Sung dynasty, had been stolen from the
delivery truck of the Sen-yung Oriental Gift
Shop on Madison Avenue.

"That's the place where Mr. Townsend bought
the vase for his wife; the one stolen during the
party!" Nancy exclaimed. "I'll bet there's some
connection between the two robberies!"

She decided to put in a long-distance call to
the gift shop the following morning and find out
if the thief had been arrested.

"He may be the same person who stole Mrs.
Townsend's vase!" Nancy cried excitedly.

Mr. Drew smiled. "Why not call the New York
police tonight?" he suggested. "I'll do it for you
if you like."

In a few minutes he had the desired information. The thief was still at large.

"How would you like to go to New York and talk to the owner of the gift shop yourself?" Mr. Drew suggested. "You'll get more information that way. Besides, you'll be able to spend a few days with Aunt Eloise."

"It's a deal!" exclaimed Nancy as she hugged her father. She had put off visiting her father's sister, Miss Eloise Drew, for far too long. "I'll catch the morning plane if I can get a reservation," she decided.

Fortunately, when she telephoned the airport, she was able to get a seat. Then she wired her aunt, telling of her time of arrival.

She slipped into bed with her head full of anticipation. New York always held a thrill for her!

Nancy was awakened the next morning by a small, cold nose sniffing her hand. She sat up to see Togo, her little fox terrier, squatting on her suitcase, his eyes fixed on her anxiously. His stubby tail began to wag while he whimpered pleadingly.

"No, Togo." Nancy yawned. "You can't come."

She rose and dressed quickly. Two hours later Nancy boarded the plane to New York. The trip was smooth and pleasant. A moment after the plane landed, Nancy saw her aunt, a tall, attractive woman of middle age.

Miss Drew, whom Nancy strikingly resembled,

possessed a charming grace which marked her as a woman of unusual intelligence.

Eloise Drew knew that Nancy was a lot like her, and secretly this gave her a thrill. Years before, when Nancy had lost her mother, Miss Drew had considered coming to live with her brother. But the private school where she taught, and in which she had a financial interest, needed her, too. When Hannah Gruen had proved so satisfactory, Miss Drew had decided to remain in New York. But she enjoyed her niece's visits immensely.

"You look wonderful, Nancy!" she said as they embraced. "And how's your father?"

"He's fine," Nancy replied, squeezing her aunt's hand.

The luncheon hour was made particularly exciting by the young detective's tale of the stolen potteries. At the end of the meal, Miss Drew readily agreed to Nancy's suggestion that they taxi to Sen-yung's Oriental Gift Shop.

Some time later their cab swung out of the heavy traffic on Madison Avenue and pulled up before the store. Nancy and her aunt stood outside a moment to admire the exotic and colorful Chinese potteries and jewelry, and odd pieces of Oriental bric-a-brac displayed in a large plate-glass window. Then they entered the shop.

Three men, one in deliveryman's uniform,

were talking at the rear of the store. One of them came forward as Nancy and her aunt entered.

Nancy hesitated. The name of the proprietor painted on the display window was Chinese, but the man who confronted her was not an Oriental.

"Is Mr. Sen-yung here?" she inquired.

The man shook his head regretfully. "Mr. Sen-yung has been at home ill for the past six weeks," he informed her. "Is there anything I can do for you? I'm John Tallow, Mr. Sen-yung's partner."

"I'm sure you can help." Nancy smiled. "Some time ago Mr. Townsend of River Heights purchased a lovely Ming vase here. I'd like to find out who sold you the vase."

"Mr. Townsend?" the man repeated slowly. "Just a moment. I'll look up the sale in my books."

He went into an office at the rear of the store. As Nancy and her aunt wandered about, examining the beautiful jewelry and porcelain, Nancy could plainly hear the other two men talking. She realized at once that one was a detective. It was evident from their conversation that the deliveryman was the driver of the truck from which the Sung tea jar had been stolen.

"I didn't get a good look at him," she heard the deliveryman say. "I'd just lifted the jar out of the truck to deliver it when I felt a gun at my back. Then a voice told me to get in the truck and drive away."

Nancy stepped forward. She apologized for the interruption and explained her interest in the case. The detective told her to ask as many questions as she wished, but there was little that the deliveryman could add to his story.

"The thief's hat was pulled down and his coat collar turned up," he said flatly. "I was too busy worrying about what he was going to do with the gun to look at him much. I did what he told me to do—left the jar on the sidewalk and scrammed!"

Nancy was disappointed not to learn more. At that moment she felt her aunt's hand on her sleeve.

"Do come and look at this vase," Miss Drew urged. "It sounds like the one you were talking about."

She led her niece to a glass cabinet off to one side of the shop. Nancy stared in amazement at the piece on display. Glazed on jade-green porcelain was a Chinese dragon in black and red.

The same design she had seen woven into the tapestry in Mr. Soong's home! The one he had said was on his stolen vase!

CHAPTER IX

Pursuit

NANCY hurried to the rear of the shop to find Mr. Tallow. Before she had a chance to ask about Mr. Soong's vase, he gave her some startling information.

"The Townsend vase," he told Nancy, "was sold to me by a Mr. David Carr."

Nancy stared at him in disbelief. David Carr! That was the name of the man her father had mentioned; the man who had vanished so mysteriously in company with the Engs!

"You're quite sure?"

"Quite." Mr. Tallow smiled pleasantly. "It's all written down in my ledger."

Nancy pointed out the dragon vase in the case. "Would you mind telling me where that came from?" she asked.

"Not at all," Mr. Tallow replied. "I bought that porcelain only yesterday from Mr. Carr."

Nancy caught her breath. She had been sure the dragon vase had been stolen from Dick's shop by John Manning. Were Carr and Manning the same person? Or had Manning sold the vase to Carr, who in turn had sold it to Sen-yung's Oriental Gift Shop?

"I'm sorry to have to tell you," Nancy said, "but this vase looks just like one that was stolen from a shop in River Heights."

Mr. Tallow's jaw dropped. "It can't be true!"

"The dragon design is exactly the same as the pattern on a Ming vase that belonged to a Mr. Soong," Nancy added.

"Mr. Soong!" the shopkeeper exclaimed. "I know him well! He is an old friend of Mr. Sen-yung! Oh, this is terrible!"

Mr. Tallow looked so worried that Nancy felt sorry for him and asked if she might examine the vase to see if it really were the same one.

"Of course, of course," he agreed.

He unlocked the cabinet door and handed the piece to Nancy. She laid the vase on its side and studied the bottom. Clearly painted on the base were several Chinese symbols. They appeared to be exactly like one set of the markings that she had found in Manning's room; the set Mr. Soong had said was on his vase.

Nancy translated the symbols. "Made in the studio of deep peace." She looked at Mr. Tallow. "Is that correct?"

He nodded nervously.

At that moment the door of the shop opened and a short, round-faced Chinese gentleman came in. He took off his hat, exposing a completely bald head, and fanned himself vigorously.

Mr. Tallow hurried toward him. "Mr. Sen-yung! Thank goodness you're back!"

After introducing his Chinese partner to Nancy, her aunt and the detective, Mr. Tallow repeated what Nancy had said about the dragon vase. Mr. Sen-yung's face became grave. Taking a magnifying glass from his pocket, he examined the pottery. Suddenly he straightened and turned to his partner.

"When did you buy this vase?" he asked sharply.

"Yesterday," Mr. Tallow replied.

"You should not have bought it without first consulting me!" Mr. Sen-yung told him heatedly.

"But you were ill!" his partner protested. "I didn't want to disturb you!" He looked at the vase, then back at the Chinese. "Is anything wrong?"

"Everything!" Mr. Sen-yung exclaimed. "This vase is a fake—an imitation!"

Mr. Tallow stared at him, dumbfounded.

"How can you tell, Mr. Sen-yung?" Nancy asked.

He showed her the barely perceptible but un-mistakable signs that had betrayed the vase to

"This vase is a fake—an imitation!"
Mr. Sen-yung exclaimed

him. Under the magnifying glass the colors showed no signs of having softened with the years, and there was a scent of newness about the porcelain. But most particularly the marks on the bottom stood out a trifle too clearly.

"It is a clever imitation," Mr. Sen-yung admitted. "Extremely expert."

Had this copy of Mr. Soong's vase been made in China and smuggled into the United States by David Carr?

Mr. Sen-yung asked his partner for the complete story of the purchase. Mr. Tallow said he had bought the dragon vase and also the one sold to Mr. Townsend from David Carr. The man had introduced himself as a sales representative of the West Coast Trading Company and shown credentials to prove his identity.

Knowing the fine reputation of the firm, Mr. Tallow had assumed the vases to be authentic. Now it seemed possible that the Townsend vase also was a fake.

"We must get the Townsend vase back at once," Mr. Sen-yung said. "If it, too, is a reproduction, we'll refund the money."

"It has been stolen," Nancy informed him. "That's really what brought me to New York." Then she asked Mr. Tallow, "What does David Carr look like?"

"He is medium height," the man replied, "with black hair and dark skin."

"Did you notice his eyes and his shoes?"

"Not his shoes," Mr. Tallow replied slowly. "But his dark eyes had a peculiar piercing stare."

"John Manning!" Nancy cried.

The two partners, Miss Eloise Drew, and the detective looked at Nancy in bewilderment. She quickly told them about the vase thief.

"Don't you see?" she finished. "Manning and Carr are probably the same man!"

"And he's the one who held up the delivery-man!" Mr. Tallow exclaimed. "I just remembered that Carr was here when I gave instructions as to when and where the jar was to be delivered."

"Did Carr say where he's staying?" Nancy asked.

"No, but I think I know where he may be," Mr. Tallow replied. "He dropped a piece of paper from his pocket. It was a letterhead from the Hotel Royalton."

Asking permission to use the office telephone, Nancy dialed the hotel. David Carr, she was told, was registered.

"If we hurry, we may catch him!"

The detective, who had been listening to Nancy's theories with great admiration, led Nancy, her aunt and Mr. Tallow to a police car in front of the store. Seconds later, they sped up Madison Avenue.

Side by side, Nancy and the detective hurried into the hotel lobby and went up to the desk.

The man showed his badge and asked for the number of David Carr's room.

The clerk looked surprised. "Mr. Carr? He just checked out."

"But I phoned only a few minutes ago," Nancy protested. "He was registered then."

"I'm sorry," the clerk told her. "He checked out right after you called."

"Did he leave any forwarding address?" she asked hopefully.

The clerk shook his head.

"Mind if we search his room?" the detective asked.

"Go ahead," the clerk replied. He took a key from the rack and gave it to the plainclothesman. "Room 414."

While Mr. Tallow waited in the lobby, to watch in case the thief should reappear, Nancy, her aunt and the detective proceeded to the room Carr had occupied.

The door was ajar. Inside, a maid was cleaning the room. The detective asked to see any scraps of paper she had picked up. The maid showed them to him. He and Nancy pored over the pieces, looking for a possible clue to Carr's whereabouts. But neither the maid's trash bag nor the room itself disclosed the slightest clue.

The detective grunted in disgust. "No use staying here. There isn't a ghost of a clue to where Carr went."

The maid stopped dusting and looked at them. "You mean the gentleman who was occupyin' this room?" she asked.

"Yes," Nancy said hopefully. "Can you tell us anything about him?"

"Well, I can tell you what I overheard," the woman replied. "Just as I came into the room to clean he was talkin' on the phone. Before he hung up, he said somethin' about meetin' somebody at the Oregon restaurant."

"Thanks!" cried Nancy.

She ran from the room, followed by her aunt and the detective. A few minutes later they joined Mr. Tallow in the lobby. Then all four taxied to the restaurant.

The Oregon was on a corner. Tingling with eagerness, Nancy almost dragged her aunt into the foyer of the narrow restaurant. The tables, she saw, were arranged along the two walls beyond a row of potted palms.

"Mr. Tallow, see if you can find Mr. Carr," she whispered. "Look through the palms."

Parting the fronds of one of the plants, he peered at the dining room. Not seeing the suspected thief, Mr. Tallow stepped into the entranceway for a better view.

"There he is!" he called excitedly.

There was a commotion at the rear of the room. Nancy saw a man spring from a chair and dash through the swinging door to the kitchen.

The detective ran in pursuit. Nancy, remembering the restaurant was situated on a corner, darted back toward the front entrance. If Carr should escape through a side door, she reasoned, he would come out around the corner.

Nancy's deduction was right. As she rounded the side of the building, Carr streaked from the restaurant's side entrance. Nancy was on his heels before the detective emerged.

The elusive Carr slipped in and out of the crowd. Pedestrians stared as Nancy raced after him.

At the corner she saw Carr dash into a subway entrance. He leaped down the steps three at a time, Nancy after him. Token in hand, he went through the turnstile like a streak of lightning.

Nancy had to pause a moment to buy a token. A train stood in the station. Carr ran forward alongside, slipping quickly into one of the forward cars.

The doors of the train were closing. Nancy leaped inside the nearest car just before the big door snapped shut. With a lurch, the crowded train started.

CHAPTER X

New Developments

NANCY was wedged tightly between the passengers as the train, with a roar, picked up speed. Reaching for a strap, she caught her breath and quickly planned her next move. She *must* push through the crowded train and find Carr!

Nancy gripped her handbag firmly and started to ease herself among the passengers. She excused herself frequently as she jostled men and women. Finally she reached the car into which the suspect had fled. Suddenly it dawned on her that she could not hold him alone. She must have help!

"I'll ask the conductor," Nancy decided, and stood on tiptoe to see if one were in sight.

As she craned her neck, she saw David Carr slouched in a seat near the far door. Near him stood the conductor. Excitedly Nancy moved forward once more.

At that moment the train started to slow for the next stop. In desperation, Nancy forged ahead. Suddenly, with a pitch that threw everybody off balance, the train jerked to an abrupt halt. The doors whipped open. Carr stepped out with the pressing crowd.

"Stop that man!" shouted Nancy. "The dark-haired one with the red tie!"

People around gaped, but no one went after him. Before Nancy herself could get to Carr, he had fled into the sea of humanity milling toward the exit.

When Nancy reached the top of the stairs, David Carr was out of sight. She searched in vain; then, disappointed, hailed a taxi to return to the Oregon restaurant.

"Nancy!" cried Miss Drew as her niece arrived. "Thank goodness you're safe. We feared Carr might have harmed you."

Nancy told her aunt and Mr. Tallow about the chase. As she finished, the detective hurried up to them. He said he had fallen over a stool that Carr had tossed at him in the kitchen. By the time he had reached the street, Carr had disappeared. Then he had searched the immediate area to no avail.

All four drove to police headquarters, where the detective made out a report on Carr. At Nancy's suggestion, they telephoned the West Coast Trading Company in San Francisco. As she had suspected, Carr had not been working for them recently.

"Your niece certainly has a good ead on her shoulders," the police captain said to Miss Eloise Drew as she and Nancy left.

"They say I'm very much like my aunt," Nancy said with a smile. "But I'm sorry we didn't catch David Carr."

Reaching the sidewalk, the Drews took a taxi to the former teacher's apartment.

Next morning Nancy suggested to her aunt that they tour Chinatown. Recalling that the stolen vases discovered in Masonville had been wrapped in Chinese newspapers, Nancy wanted to go to the office of the *China Daily Times* and make some inquiries.

When the two reached Mott Street, they located the newspaper office and went inside. Nancy asked a pleasant man the names of subscribers in Masonville and River Heights. He willingly told her, but neither John Manning nor David Carr was among them.

"Nothing came of that hunch," Nancy told her aunt as they headed for a fine Chinese restaurant.

As they finished a delicious seven-course meal, Aunt Eloise gave her niece a worried look. "Wouldn't it be wise to give up the case and stay out of Carr's way, dear?" she suggested.

Nancy patted her aunt's hand reassuringly. "Don't worry about me, Aunt Eloise. I promise to be doubly careful. Anyway, I'm going home tomorrow and maybe he'll stay here."

Actually the young detective felt that if Carr and Manning were the same person, there was a good possibility he was already on his way back to the River Heights area. She would have to watch her step!

"You're going home?" her aunt repeated. "Oh, Nancy, I thought—"

"Sorry, darling," her niece said. "A friend of Ned's is being married. Ned's to be an usher. I promised to drive up to Emerson and get him day after tomorrow."

"I hate to have you leave," her aunt said wistfully. "But I bow to the younger generation! Now let's do some sightseeing."

The following day, on arriving home, she was welcomed by a smiling Hannah Gruen and a barking, tail-wagging Togo.

Ned telephoned just as Nancy started to unpack. Nancy plunged into a brief description of her activities.

"Wow!" he exclaimed when she finished. "You sound like a one-woman police force! Anyway, I'm glad you're back. I'd begun to think you'd forgotten about me."

"Not a chance!" she assured the youth. "I'll be at Emerson tomorrow by twelve o'clock."

"Okay."

Later, Nancy called Mr. Soong. The Chinese gentleman was shocked to hear that an imitation of his rare Ming vase had been sold to the Senyung Oriental Gift Shop. He congratulated Nancy on her brave attempt to capture Carr and expressed the hope that the man would be apprehended soon.

The next day when Nancy arrived at Ned's fraternity house she was immediately surrounded by the various members. Having attended many parties there, she was well known and well liked.

"Ned's not here," one teased. "Prof kept him after class. How about lunch with me?"

"Say, you big so-and-so," called a youth, clattering down the stairs. "Lay off!"

Ned appeared, grinning, turned Nancy around and marched her back to the car. They had lunch at an attractive inn, then started for Ned's home, a few miles out of River Heights. On the way, Nancy gave Ned all the details of her search for a China clay pit near the leaning chimney. While they were going through Masonville, she suddenly asked Ned to stop.

"What's up?" Ned asked.

They were in front of the courthouse.

"I've been wanting to find out who owns that fenced-in property in the woods," Nancy replied. "Let's go in to ask the Registrar of Deeds."

Ned followed her up the steps and into the

registrar's office. The clerk handed them a map and ledger. Together they flipped the pages until they came to the entry Nancy was seeking.

The records showed that a tract of land comprising some two hundred and fifty acres, including the abandoned Civil War mine, had been purchased by Miles Monroe of Philadelphia five years ago.

"Miles Monroe!" Nancy exclaimed in surprise. "That's where he said he came from!"

"Who's he?" Ned inquired.

"A geologist I went to see about the China clay pit. Now I know why Mr. Monroe asked me to let him know if I located it."

"Sounds phony to me," Ned declared. "Want to stop and see him?"

"If you have time."

"I'm not due at the bachelor dinner until seven-thirty. So let's go. I'd like to see this Mr. Monroe and ask him what he means by trying to put one over on the world's prettiest detective."

"Ned, stop it!" Nancy commanded.

They left the courthouse and drove to Miles Monroe's apartment in River Heights. As before, an eye stared through the peephole in answer to Nancy's ring. When the professor recognized Nancy, the door flew open.

"Glad you called," he said. "I have something to show you. But first, tell me why you came."

Nancy introduced Ned, then quickly got to the

problem on her mind. "We've found out your secret, Professor Monroe!"

"My secret?" he asked, perplexed.

"It's you who owns the old iron mine!"

"Me?" exclaimed the geologist. Then he burst out laughing. "I never owned a piece of land in my life!"

"The property is listed as being owned by Miles Monroe of Philadelphia," Nancy told him. "Who could this Miles Monroe be?"

The professor shook his head. "Search me!" he snorted. "To the best of my knowledge I was the only Miles Monroe in Philadelphia."

Nancy felt sure the man was telling the truth. Since he could tell her nothing more, she put the puzzling question aside for the moment.

"You said you had something to show me," she reminded him.

The geologist uncrossed his long, bony legs and limped over to the bookcase. He took out a thick volume that looked to be very old. Carefully he turned the pages to a place he had marked.

"After you told me you were searching for a China clay deposit," the professor said, "I came across a reference in this old book on geology."

With Ned looking on, Nancy read the paragraph the geologist had marked. It told of a fine white clay that had been found one mile southeast of a "crook in Huntsman's River" during the days of the early settlers.

"Huntsman's River?" Nancy said. "Why, that must be Hunter's Creek. That's the stream which runs under Hunter's Bridge."

"Exactly! And the clay the book describes is China clay, or I'm no geologist!"

"Thank you so much, Professor Monroe," said Nancy, rising to depart.

Ned shook hands with the geologist. "Nice to meet you, sir," he said. "This sounds like a good clue for Nancy."

When the couple reached the car, Ned suggested that they spend the next afternoon following the directions to the China clay pit.

"And how about Mrs. Gruen packing one of those super picnic lunches?" he added with a grin.

Nancy laughed. "It's a date."

At twelve the next day they started out. Nancy told Ned she had learned that no Miles Monroe was listed in the Philadelphia telephone directory. Her father had obtained this information.

"It's sure a mystery," declared Ned. "But maybe we'll soon clear it up."

Reaching Hunter's Bridge, Nancy showed him where to park and they locked the car. Taking the picnic basket, they started off, following the water upstream for a mile to a point where it swerved sharply.

"This must be the 'crook' the book mentioned," Ned said. "How about eating?"

Nancy nodded. She squinted at the position of

the sun, then pointed to the left. "And southeast should be in that direction."

Half an hour later the two explorers, their appetites well satisfied, set off once more. When they had gone exactly one mile, as the directions had indicated, Nancy stopped.

"The clay should be near here!"

"Say, what's this?" Ned exclaimed, bending down to examine a little gully. "Do you suppose this is part of the old clay pit?"

The two stepped into the depression, overgrown with weeds and brush. As they did, Ned kicked against a piece of flat, corroded iron.

"Probably part of an old forge," he remarked.

"Just what we need!" Nancy exclaimed. "We can use it as a shovel."

"For what?" Ned queried.

"To dig with," Nancy replied, pointing to the bottom of the gully.

Ned dug. Finally he said ruefully, "Nothing here but a lot of gravel. This isn't a China clay pit. It's only—"

He stopped speaking as a wild cry pierced the woods some distance ahead. It sounded like *bong*.

"Someone's in trouble!" Nancy exclaimed, starting to run.

A few moments later she and Ned emerged into a clearing. To Nancy's utter astonishment, the four-walled enclosure of boards confronted her!

CHAPTER XI

The Impostor

HAD the cry come from inside the mysterious enclosure? Nancy ran eagerly toward the fence and listened. There was not a sound.

"How do we get inside?" Ned asked, anxious to help the person in distress.

"There's no opening," Nancy told him. "I wish we could climb over."

"At least we can look over," said Ned, pointing to a stout tree limb lying on the ground. "If you'll help me, we can prop this against the fence for a ladder, Nancy."

Together they lugged the limb across the clearing and lifted it against the fence.

"You go up while I hold it," Ned suggested.

Nancy placed her hands around the bough and, monkey-fashion, started up.

"What do you see?" Ned asked as she reached the top.

"Not much. Trees. Lots of them." She scampered down. "But we're not far from the leaning chimney. Let's go over there and take a look."

Ned willingly dragged the tree limb the short distance and Nancy climbed up again. Below her was the rectangular enclosure, a stone wall, and the battered brick building she had seen some days before through a knothole.

Glancing up, Nancy was startled to find that the rusted ornament on the leaning chimney was gone. She looked at the ground below, thinking the symbol had dropped off. It was not there.

"Say, what's so interesting?" Ned called up.

"Come on up."

Nancy told him about the missing ornament, and also Bess's declaration that she had seen a hand sticking from the chimney. Maybe someone *had* climbed up inside, planning to remove the iron coat of arms, or whatever it was.

"This place gets more mysterious every day," Nancy remarked.

"It's funny there's no sign of life around, though," Ned commented. "You'd think somebody—"

He stopped speaking as they heard a far-off cry. Again it sounded like *bong,* and again it was impossible to tell whether the call of distress had come from inside the enclosure.

Almost simultaneously with the cry came the menacing crack of rotted wood.

"The tree limb!" Nancy cried. Nancy and Ned scurried down just as the old limb split.

Ned helped Nancy to her feet. "No more sleuthing today," he insisted. "Anyway, I can just about make that wedding rehearsal in time."

Nancy hated to leave so soon but said nothing. They trekked back to the car and Ned drove to his home in Mapleton, a suburb of River Heights.

"See you tomorrow afternoon at the wedding," he said, getting out. "And don't let any other usher take you up the aisle!"

Nancy laughingly promised. Then, as she drove on to River Heights, her thoughts turned again to the enclosure in the woods. Both leads which Miles Monroe had given her, the one to the old iron mine and the directions along Hunter's Creek, had led to the strange spot in the woods.

Was the China clay inside? Did the owner know about it? Nancy set her chin in determination. She would find out! And soon!

Hannah Gruen met her at the rear door of the Drew home, her kindly face lined with worry.

"What's wrong?" Nancy asked quickly.

"Oh, Nancy, Mr. Soong has been phoning you for the past half hour! He's terribly upset! He's at police headquarters!"

"What for?"

"I don't know," the housekeeper answered, "but I think he's in trouble."

Nancy ran down the porch steps to her car. She drove rapidly, wondering at every turn what the police could want with gentle Mr. Soong!

Nancy ran into police headquarters. The old Chinese gentleman was sitting dejectedly in Chief McGinnis's office. Nancy looked from Mr. Soong to the police officer, then back to Mr. Soong.

"What happened?" she asked.

Mr. Soong, his face lighting at the sight of the young detective, opened his mouth to speak. Chief McGinnis intervened quietly.

"Perhaps I'd better explain," he told Nancy. He picked up a paper from his desk. "I received this report today from the New York City police. A woman in New York, named Mrs. Marsden, has complained that a Chinese vase she bought is a fake. She claims it was sold to her by a Mr. Soong of River Heights. She mailed him money orders for five hundred dollars, which he cashed." The officer looked up, adding:

"We've checked with the postal clerk in Masonville. His description of the man who collected the money tallies exactly with that of Mr. Soong."

The Chinese turned despairing eyes on Nancy. "I know nothing about it," he said. "Surely you believe me?"

"Of course!" Nancy said emphatically. "Chief McGinnis, does the report give a description of the vase?"

The officer scanned the paper. "Yes, it does."

The young detective's pulse quickened with eagerness. She was playing a hunch. If it worked, everything would be straightened out!

"Does it say that the vase is brown," Nancy rushed on, "with a pattern showing an old Chinese sitting beside a deer under a peach tree at the edge of a blue lake?"

Chief McGinnis stared. "Why, yes!"

"And does it say the Chinese markings on the bottom of the vase mean 'Made for the hall of fragrant virtue'?"

The police officer's jaw dropped. "How did you know all that?" he demanded.

"Because that vase," Nancy replied evenly, "is the one stolen from the Townsends' home. I saw it there the night it was taken!"

"Well," Chief McGinnis said, "this is a new angle."

"What's more," Nancy continued, "Mr. Soong couldn't have been the thief because I measured the thief's footprints in the flower bed. They were short and wide. And as you can clearly see, Mr. Soong's feet are narrow!"

She paused for breath, and McGinnis wiped his forehead. He sat for a moment, considering, while Nancy watched him anxiously.

"That puts a different complexion on the case," the officer said at last. "But how do you explain the fact that the postal clerk's description of the man who cashed the money orders fits Mr. Soong?"

Nancy deliberated. "The thief probably wore a disguise so he could pass as Mr. Soong," she said finally. "It wouldn't be difficult—a pair of spectacles and a tiny goatee. He must have stolen some means of identification and forged Mr. Soong's signature to the money orders."

"You may possibly be right," the chief said, "but just the same I think I'll drive Mr. Soong over to Masonville, to see that postal clerk. Want to come, Nancy?"

"Yes, indeed."

"We'll go there in my car."

Late that afternoon Nancy, Mr. Soong, and the chief arrived at the Masonville post office. At Nancy's suggestion, the two men stayed out of sight while she went to the money-order window.

Nancy introduced herself to the clerk, then listened carefully as he described the man who had collected the money for the fake vase. His description corresponded exactly with that of Mr. Soong.

"You're quite sure you would recognize the man if you saw him again?" she asked.

"I'm positive!" the clerk told her confidently. "It isn't often that I cash orders for five hundred dollars, so I pay particular attention to anybody collecting that amount of money."

Nancy beckoned to Mr. Soong and had him stand facing the clerk. Chief McGinnis looked on approvingly.

"Is this the man?" she asked.

The clerk stared at the Chinese gentleman.

"That's the one, all right!" he declared. "I'd know him anywhere!"

Nancy thought quickly. There had to be *some* way in which she could prove to the clerk he was mistaken. She took a money-order application form and gave it to Mr. Soong, together with a pen.

"Please fill it out," she told her friend. Then she said to the clerk, "Perhaps you've overlooked something. Some small detail—"

She broke off as the clerk's eyes widened in watching Mr. Soong write.

"Hey, wait a minute, there is something wrong!" he said. "The Chinese I gave the money to signed his name with his right hand. This gentleman writes with his left hand."

"Then he can't be the same man!" Nancy stated triumphantly.

The clerk shook his head. "No, he can't," he admitted slowly. "In fact," he added, "this man speaks better English. I hadn't thought of that before. But the two of 'em look alike."

Chief McGinnis said he was sorry to have put Mr. Soong in such an embarrassing position.

They drove back to River Heights, and Nancy took the elderly Chinese home in her car.

"How can I ever repay you?" Mr. Soong said.

"By telling me more someday about your country's beautiful pottery," Nancy said, smiling.

He insisted she come inside at once to be presented with a little gift in token of his gratitude.

As she accompanied the Chinese toward his door, it suddenly swung open. In the entrance stood Mr. Soong's Chinese servant, Ching. His small, inscrutable eyes for once were wide with surprise. Then his lips parted in a toothy smile and he spoke rapidly in Chinese, gesticulating all the while.

Mr. Soong replied in the same tongue. Ching turned to Nancy, his smile growing bigger. Again he spoke.

"What is he saying?" she asked Mr. Soong.

"Ching is thanking you for delivering me from the hands of the police," he explained.

Mr. Soong chuckled. Then he disappeared for a moment, returning with a bottle of delicate wisteria perfume imported from China.

"It is little for me to do." He bowed when Nancy thanked him for the gift.

"I'll wear some of it to the wedding I'm going to tomorrow afternoon," she said.

"Miss Tyson's wedding?" the Chinese inquired. "Perhaps I shall see you there."

The next day, after the church ceremony,

Nancy and her friends drove to the reception at the bride's home. After wishing the couple every happiness and having punch and party sandwiches, Nancy and Ned went to admire the many lovely wedding gifts displayed in an upstairs room.

Mr. Soong walked in directly behind them. Almost at once, the man's eyes fell on a Chinese porcelain jewel box. He picked it up with a pleased exclamation.

"It's beautiful!" said Nancy.

The porcelain jewel case was decorated with plum blossoms. They were painted on a background of deep-blue water lightly coated with cracking ice.

As Mr. Soong started to replace the jewel box, his eyes suddenly bulged, and he exclaimed in Chinese.

"What is it?" Nancy asked quickly.

Mr. Soong pointed with a shaking finger to two Chinese symbols worked into the blossoms. They were the same strange symbols Nancy had seen concealed in the peach-tree pattern on the Townsends' vase!

She turned again to Mr. Soong. The elderly gentleman's lips were parted. He seemed unable to take his eyes from the symbols.

"What are they?" she asked.

"They are the marks of Eng Moy!" he whispered. "My missing friend Eng Moy!"

CHAPTER XII

A Jade Elephant

"ENG MOY!" Nancy gasped.

Mr. Soong nodded slowly, as if he still could not believe it himself. "I would know my friend's signature anywhere."

"But I don't understand," Nancy said. "If Eng Moy made the jewel box, why didn't he sign his name on the bottom? Why did he work it into the design where it can barely be seen?"

"That I myself do not understand."

Mr. Soong turned the box bottom up. Several Chinese characters were painted on the base.

"It is from the Wan Li period, the last great epoch of art in the Ming dynasty," Mr. Soong stated. "Eng Moy did not make the vase. So he could not have put his initials on it."

"There's no question that the box is authentic?" Nancy asked.

"Why do you ask?"

Nancy told the Chinese about the two symbols that were Eng Moy's signature concealed in the design of the Townsends' vase. "That piece—the one sold to Mrs. Marsden in New York City—was an imitation of an old vase," she added.

Mr. Soong stared at Nancy in hurt bewilderment. She decided to avoid offending him further. But she wanted to explore the possible link between Eng Moy and the swindler David Carr.

"Perhaps if I learn where this jewel box came from, it will help us find the Engs," she said.

Mr. Soong's face lit up. "A splendid idea!"

Nancy wandered about among the wedding guests until she found the bride's mother. Then she asked discreetly if she knew where the attractive old jewel box had come from.

"Why, Mrs. Dareff gave my daughter the box," the hostess said kindly. "It came from that lovely antique shop in Westville."

Nancy knew the store and its proprietor. She made a beeline for the telephone, Ned close by.

"A swell way to enjoy a reception!" he grumbled in mock disapproval as Nancy dialed.

"As soon as I finish this call," she promised, "we'll go have some more refreshments."

"You're on!" He grinned. "And furthermore, we're going from the reception direct to the country club. There's a dance tonight, and some of us have fixed up a little party."

"Fine," Nancy beamed. "Hello? . . . Mrs.

Lorimer? . . . This is Nancy Drew of River Heights."

She told the owner of the shop where she was, then asked about the jewel case.

"Isn't it lovely?" the woman effused. "Now let me see— Oh, yes, I purchased that piece several weeks ago from Mr. David Carr."

"Was he a man of medium height with rather piercing eyes? Is he from San Francisco?" Nancy asked.

"Why, yes. You know him?"

"I've heard of him. He's a thief, Mrs. Lorimer. If he should show up again, will you please tell the police right away?"

At that instant Bess Marvin rushed up to Nancy. "Come on! Quick!"

Nancy said good-by to Mrs. Lorimer and hung up.

"The bride's going to throw her bouquet," Bess said excitedly. "Don't *you* want to catch it?" she asked, glancing sidewise at Ned.

Nancy blushed and rushed away to where eager hands hoped to catch the symbolic "next to be married" bouquet. But she stayed in the background. The maid of honor caught the white roses.

While waiting for the bride to change to traveling clothes and come downstairs, Nancy noticed some guests she had not seen before. There were Dick Milton and his wife Connie. Joining the couple, she learned they had just arrived. Dick had not been able to get away from his shop, and Connie had had no one with whom to leave the baby.

"Sue's outside in her carriage," Connie explained, after being introduced.

"It's a shame you missed the wedding," Nancy declared. "Please let me know when you want to go out. I'll be glad to baby-sit for you."

"That's awfully sweet of you, Nancy. I hate to take you up on it right away, but are you free on the nineteenth?" Connie asked.

"Yes. I'll come over."

"I'd love to go to a luncheon party that day," Connie explained. "Dick's going out of town to see about some different kind of clay."

"Not China clay," Dick spoke up quietly. "You haven't had any luck, Nancy?"

She told him of her recent search and how both of Miles Monroe's clues to the China clay pit had led to the mysterious enclosure in the woods.

"The first chance I have I'll go out there."

"I hope you'll find the clay," Dick replied. "The sooner I repay Mr. Soong the better, and there's not much chance of my doing it unless something big comes my way."

"The bride's ready to leave!" an excited girl called out, and paper rose petals were tossed at the bride and groom as they hurried down the stairs and through the hall to the front porch. Then a car door banged, and the couple were off on their honeymoon.

Ned found Nancy, and after saying good-by to their host and hostess, they left for the country club with a group of friends.

Later, when the dance was over, Ned helped Nancy into the car and slid in behind the wheel to drive home.

"Let's take the Three Bridges Road," she said.

"Do you expect to find Manning-Carr at Hunter's Bridge?" he asked teasingly.

"Well, things seem to happen there," Nancy replied. "He may use it as a meeting place."

Ned swung the convertible onto Three Bridges Road and drove swiftly toward River Heights. When the car approached the twisting turns, Ned pressed on the brake and coasted. As they slowly rounded the final curve in the series of turns, Nancy stared intently at the underbrush a short distance back from the road. At the spot where she had previously seen a man's footprints, she now saw only the black shadows of the night.

Nancy turned her attention to the opposite side of the road, while the car continued slowly toward Hunter's Bridge.

Suddenly, behind some bushes at the edge of the creek where it curved under the bridge, Nancy saw the small white glow of a flashlight.

"Look!" She pointed excitedly, then took her own flashlight from the front compartment of the car. "Stop!" she told Ned. "Let's investigate!"

They got out and crept down the embankment toward the light Nancy had seen. The couple stepped carefully, avoiding twigs and stones that might make a sound and betray their presence.

As they neared the shrubs, the light went out. Nancy and Ned hardly dared to breathe, but they saw no one.

Finally Nancy beamed her flashlight ahead. The next moment she had kicked off her shoes and was wading into the water.

"What—!" Ned exclaimed.

Nancy was soon on the other side of the narrow, shallow stream. She swooped up something from the ground and played her flashlight beam on it.

"What is it?" Ned called.

She held up the object, a green jade elephant about three inches long and two inches high.

"How'd that get here?" Ned asked.

"Someone just dropped it," Nancy replied, "and I don't believe he meant to."

"I'll come over and help you find him," Ned offered. "Is the elephant any good?"

As Nancy was about to say she thought it was Mr. Soong's valuable jade piece, there came the roar of a motor.

"My car!" Nancy cried out, and ran back across the stream.

Slipping into her shoes, she dashed after Ned, who was already halfway up the embankment. Two feet from the top of the slope they knew the worst.

Nancy's convertible was speeding away into the night!

CHAPTER XIII

A Bold Plan

NANCY and Ned stood aghast as the car's tail-light finally disappeared.

"Well, if I'm not a nitwit!" Ned said. "If I had locked the car this wouldn't have happened. We'd better run to a telephone and notify the police," he added. "A state trooper can overtake your car."

Nancy smiled wanly. "I'm afraid we'll be too late, Ned," she replied. "The nearest phone is about two miles from here."

The youth frowned. "I guess our best chance is to thumb a ride," he said at last. "Maybe a driver will give us a lift to town in time to do some good."

But Nancy knew there was small chance of anyone driving through the lonely stretch of woods at that hour. She and Ned started hiking toward River Heights, Nancy clutching the jade elephant.

Ned looked very forlorn and incongruous in his formal clothes, with a white carnation on his lapel. Nancy's high-heeled shoes were uncomfortable on the rough road, and her stockings were still wet from her dash through the creek.

After trudging two miles, the couple came to a gas station, where Nancy telephoned the State Police. The officer said he would notify all patrol cars to be on the lookout. Then he promised to send a trooper to take Nancy and Ned to their homes.

Nancy said nothing about the jade elephant, wishing to present it to Mr. Soong or Dick herself.

"Nancy," Ned said as they reached her house, "I'm due to go back to college early tomorrow morning, but I think I'll stick around here and help hunt for your car."

"No, you go on back to Emerson," she insisted. "I have an idea the person who took my car will abandon it somewhere. It'll turn up."

But next morning Nancy learned that the police had not found the convertible. When she went into the dining room, her father was finishing his breakfast.

"Dad, I'm worried," she announced. "So far the police haven't found a single trace of my car. I guess it's gone for good!"

Togo frisked into the room and barked cheerfully at his mistress. Mr. Drew looked thoughtfully at his daughter as she absently scratched the terrier's ears.

"Any idea who took the car?" he asked at last.

"I'm almost certain Manning-Carr or someone he was going to meet is the thief," she answered.

The lawyer took a sip of coffee. "You're probably right," he agreed. "And I don't like the situation. I've done some more checking on Carr."

"Tell me about him," Nancy said, pushing her concern about the stolen car out of her mind.

"I learned from the authorities in Washington," Mr. Drew went on, "that he's wanted for smuggling and a dozen other offenses. Seems he's of mixed blood."

"Part Chinese?" Nancy interrupted.

"His mother was Chinese. He's American on his father's side. In appearance, Carr is supposed to resemble his father."

"Oh!" Nancy said excitedly. "Now I'm beginning to put two and two together."

"And that's not all the story," said her father. "Carr has a brother who's also reported to be a criminal. But he's too cunning for anything definite to be known about him. He may be in the Orient or he may be in the United States; the authorities aren't sure which."

"Does he look like Carr?" Nancy asked quickly.

"No," the lawyer replied, "he looks like a Chinese."

Nancy mulled over this information. She was

sure now the brother was working with Carr. That would account for the second set of footprints which had baffled her. It also would account for the person who had cashed the money orders made out to Mr. Soong.

"Carr's brother may be hiding in the enclosure in the woods," she said to herself after her father had left the house. "Even Carr may be there!"

Nancy determined that as soon as she returned the jade elephant, she would investigate the enclosure. She would ask if Bess or George could use the family automobile and drive her there. This time she was going to find out why the fence had been built!

Hannah Gruen insisted upon knowing what Nancy was planning. She thought it might be dangerous and felt it was her duty to warn Nancy.

"You may be trespassing on property that doesn't concern the mystery," she pointed out. "Innocent people may live there, and they would have a perfect right to guard their property from intrusion."

Nancy hugged the faithful housekeeper. "If something happens to me, I know you'll come to the rescue!"

As Nancy walked to the telephone, Mrs. Gruen smiled. She knew that the young detective was determined to solve the mystery, but that she would not do anything foolhardy.

Neither Mr. Soong nor his servant Ching answered the telephone, so Nancy dialed Dick Milton's shop.

"Hold everything, Dick!" she said. "I've found the stolen jade elephant."

"No fooling!"

She asked him if he wanted to return the article to Mr. Soong personally.

"You found the elephant. Please take it to Mr. Soong."

Nancy agreed and carefully concealed the piece in a drawer of the dressing table in her bedroom. She would take the jade piece to Mr. Soong later.

Humming cheerfully at the prospect of finding the key to the mystery of the enclosure in the woods, Nancy set out for Bess Marvin's house. Her plump friend and George were putting golf balls on the lawn. Nancy described the events of the night before and the girls listened with astonishment.

"So I'm looking for a driver to take me to the mystery enclosure," she said in conclusion.

"Again?" Bess gasped. "I don't like that place."

"Oh, don't be a ninny," George retorted.

"All right," Bess agreed reluctantly. "I'll ask Mother if we can take the car."

After a few minutes she reappeared and said she could have it late that afternoon. It was four o'clock when they started off. This time they tied a ladder to the top of the car.

Bess headed for Three Bridges Road. A short time later they parked the car and the three girls started off through the woods, carrying the ladder.

When they finally saw the familiar four-walled wooden enclosure in the clearing before them, they paused to rest. The mysterious compound was strangely silent.

Bess looked apprehensive. "Oh, Nancy, I don't like it!" she whispered. "Let's go back!"

"Don't be a silly!" George scolded her cousin.

Bess subsided uncomfortably, with nervous glances at the surrounding area. Nancy and George picked up the ladder and the three walked on. Passing the knoll near the leaning chimney, Nancy decided to take a look from there.

"Bess, maybe you were right!" Nancy exclaimed. "Maybe someone *did* reach a hand out of the chimney! There's a new symbol up there now!"

The cousins rushed to Nancy's side and stared in amazement. Nancy, puzzled, told them that the original iron ornament was missing when she and Ned had looked at the chimney.

"This new one," she said, taking a pencil and pad from her clutch bag, "is like the other one, only it has more crosspieces."

"Looks like an Oriental ornament of some sort," George remarked.

Nancy said nothing. She asked the others to help her prop the ladder against the fence, then nimbly climbed it.

The scene inside the enclosure was exactly the same as when she had viewed it with Ned. There was little to be seen because of trees and bushes.

Climbing down, Nancy suggested they move the ladder to a part of the fence over which she had not looked before. The girls carried it to the end of the enclosure opposite the leaning chimney.

Once more Nancy surveyed the grounds.

"See anything?" Bess demanded.

Nancy glanced down and shook her head.

"Maybe people just come here once in a while," George ventured.

"They go in and out all right," Nancy said, and added excitedly, "Girls, I see the entrance gate!"

"Where?" George asked.

"Not far from here. It's very cleverly constructed so it doesn't show from the outside."

She had barely uttered this statement, when Nancy's attention became fixed.

"Someone's coming!" she announced. "A strange-looking person!"

Coming toward Nancy among the trees of the wooden enclosure was a tall woman dressed in a flowing lavender robe. Over her head she wore a hood of the same color. Encircling her waist was a knotted rope, the ends of which dangled as far down as her sandaled feet. She stared at the girl perched on the ladder.

"Get down from there at once!" she ordered.

Going to the gate, she lifted the iron latch and pulled open the cleverly concealed gate. Nancy scrambled down the ladder just as the woman appeared outside the fence. She came rapidly toward the three girls.

"What are you doing here?" she demanded.

"We didn't mean any harm—" Bess stammered, but Nancy interrupted her.

"We're searching for something," she explained with a friendly smile. "We were looking to see if it might be on the other side of the fence."

"You have no right to spy on our grounds!" the woman retorted sharply. "Go away and never return!"

Bess tugged at Nancy's sleeve. "Come on!"

Nancy ignored her friend's suggestion.

"We'll leave as soon as we learn what we came to find out," she said.

The woman's eyes narrowed. "What do you want to know?" she asked after a moment.

"We're searching for a pit of China clay," Nancy told her. "We have reason to believe it's in this vicinity. Can you tell us anything about it?"

The woman's hands clenched below the long, wide sleeves of her robe.

"I know of no such thing. Heed my warning and never come back!"

George, who had been staring at her long, hooded robe, asked suddenly, "Are you a member of a religious sect?"

"I belong to the Lavender Sisters," the woman replied. "The gardens beyond that wall are sacred. Those who dare defy us and trespass will be tormented by evil spirits until the day they die!"

Bess turned to Nancy appealingly, but the detective was not yet ready to go.

"Do Oriental women live here with you?"

The Lavender Sister gave Nancy a searching look. "No. Why do you ask?"

"Because of the symbol on the chimney," Nancy replied.

"The symbol?" the woman asked, puzzled. Then she added quickly, "Oh, yes, the symbol. I had forgotten."

She gave no further explanation, and again ordered the girls away.

"Help me carry the ladder, George," Nancy said.

With Nancy carrying one end of the ladder and George the other, the girls started back through the woods. The woman watched them for a while, then she quickly re-entered the wooden enclosure and latched the gate behind her.

"What a strange place for a religious colony," Bess said, ducking under a low-hanging branch.

"Go away and never return!" the woman ordered

"I'm not convinced it *is* a religious colony," Nancy replied.

"Me neither!" George declared. "Most of the things the woman said sounded like a lot of mumbo jumbo! I think she's funny in the head!"

"You can't tell," Bess observed seriously. "I'm just as glad we're going away from the place."

"Say!" George exclaimed when they reached a dirt lane. "This isn't the way we came, but maybe it connects with the gravel road."

They had gone about two hundred feet when Nancy stopped short and stared fixedly at something directly ahead of them in a small clearing.

It was Nancy's car!

"Hypers!" George cried in disbelief.

The girls dropped the ladder and rushed forward. The convertible was undamaged.

Nancy opened the door and looked inside the car. Everything was just as she had left it, but the ignition switch was locked and the keys were missing. On the floor lay an old pair of elevator shoes.

Nancy turned and faced her friends.

"I don't know about you two," she declared, "but I'm going back to the enclosure and get inside! It's no coincidence that we've found my car and these shoes here. I'm sure the car was stolen by some friend of Manning-Carr, and I'll bet that enclosure is their hideout."

"That's why the Lavender Sister didn't want

us around," George added. "I'll go back with you, Nancy, and see what we can find out."

"But we mustn't get caught," Bess warned.

The sunlight was hidden by an overcast as the girls again emerged from among the trees and went toward the fence. Nancy placed the ladder in a different spot from where she had put it before and quickly climbed to the top.

"Keep watch!" she whispered. "I'll come out the gate."

It took only a moment to break the rusted strands of barbed wire. Then, taking a final look to make certain she was unobserved, the young sleuth carefully dropped the ten feet down inside the enclosure.

She crept cautiously to the edge of a clearing. To the right was the stone wall and the front of the old brick building with the leaning chimney.

Just as Nancy had decided to leave the concealment of the shrubs, she saw the Lavender Sister come through a small wooden door in the stone wall. At her side trotted a huge mastiff!

Nancy moved back farther into the bushes, hoping that her movements would go undetected in the failing light. The huge dog raised his head as if listening but did not look in her direction.

The woman with the mastiff strode toward the gate in the fence. As they came closer to Nancy, she saw that the dog was held by a long chain attached to his collar.

Nancy watched with sudden apprehension as the woman went up to the gate. Suppose she should leave the enclosure? She would surely see Bess and George waiting outside!

But luck favored the girls. Stepping to one side of the gate, the Lavender Sister hooked the leash to an iron ring attached to one of the boards. Leaving the mastiff to stand watch, she started back toward the brick building.

So relieved was Nancy at her friends' escape from detection, she had not given any thought to her own plight. But as her eyes returned to the mastiff, the truth struck her with sickening force.

She could neither do any investigating without attracting the dog's attention, nor could she leave the wooden enclosure by way of the gate!

Indeed, she dared not make the slightest sign or sound that would betray her presence to the mastiff and set him to baying an alarm.

She was trapped!

CHAPTER XIV

Mad Dash!

NANCY felt a wave of panic, but she swiftly steeled her nerves. Now was the time for cool reasoning, she told herself, not a surrender to sudden fears.

"If I go in the other direction, away from the dog, maybe he won't detect me," she decided. "I'll worry later about getting out of here."

Nancy tiptoed along, making her way to the old brick building. Not a sound could be heard from within. She tried the door. It was locked.

Suddenly lights sprang up behind some distant trees and spread a low white glow over the area. A moment later a red glare flared up briefly and Nancy could hear indistinct voices.

Presently there was a clink of metal, the rattle of a chain. Then an engine sputtered, coughed, and finally settled down to a steady chug-chug-chug.

"What's that for?" Nancy wondered. "It might

123

be a water pump, but why all the lights?"

Starting forward, she suddenly found her path blocked. Two Lavender Sisters came out of the shadows. One stood as if guarding the unseen operation. The other walked briskly toward the mastiff. Nancy recognized her as the woman she had encountered earlier.

The dog rose at her approach, and the woman placed a large tin pan heaped with raw meat in front of him. As the dog's jaws crunched into the meat, the Lavender Sister turned to go back. At that moment in a low but clearly audible voice from outside the high board fence came a call.

"Nancy!"

It was Bess's voice!

She called again, even more anxiously. "Nancy! Where are you?"

Nancy longed to reply, but more fervently than that she wished Bess would stop calling, because the woman was staring in the direction of the voice.

Hastily Nancy tiptoed nearer the fence. Taking a notebook from her bag, she quickly scribbled a warning:

"Hide!"

She tore off the page and wrapped it around a stone, which she tossed over the fence. She hoped Bess or George would see it. Then she looked again toward the woman.

The Lavender Sister seemed to be hesitating,

not certain whether to investigate or not. Then, with sudden decision, she walked to the gate and pushed up the latch.

"The ladder!" Nancy remembered wildly.

What if the girls had left it propped against the fence and the woman instigated a search of the grounds to see who had climbed over!

As the long-robed figure slipped outside the wooden enclosure, Nancy waited with bated breath for the outcome of the woman's search. Seconds dragged into minutes, but there was no sound. Finally the Lavender Sister reappeared inside the grounds and shut the gate behind her.

Nancy gave a sigh of relief. Taking the ladder with them, the girls had apparently hidden in the nearby woods.

Nancy's hope of seeing more of the grounds to learn if there were a China clay pit, or to locate Manning-Carr or his brother, faded as time went on. The two Lavender Sisters stood in stony silence, barring all chance to do this. Finally Nancy concluded she would have to give up and try to get out of the place.

"But that awful beast!" she told herself.

The mastiff uttered a low, throaty growl as if he sensed an alien presence. Nancy scribbled a second note to Bess and George, briefly describing her plight. After folding the paper around a stone, she tossed the note over the fence.

But neither a note nor the sound of a voice

came over the top of the wooden partition in reply.

Nancy was worried. "I hope they didn't run into any trouble."

This thought spurred her on to seek an escape from the enclosure and find out what had happened to them.

The dog stretched himself on the ground beside the gate, his massive head resting quietly but watchfully between his paws. Nancy looked at him and bit her lip in vexation.

"Guess there's only one thing to do," she reflected. "That's to wait until somebody comes and takes the brute away."

An hour passed, Nancy hoping against hope. Apparently the dog had been stationed beside the gate for the night.

A bold plan half formed in her mind, and she searched the ground along the fence until she found a rock beneath a shrub.

"It's dark enough now," she decided.

She stole stealthily among the trees and bushes in the direction of the dog. When about fifty feet from him, she stopped and took stock of her position. The ground that separated her from the dog was bare.

She weighed the small rock in her hand. Then she carefully approximated the length of the dog's leash.

"Here's hoping!" she murmured. Aiming at a

spot on the fence, Nancy let the rock fly with unerring accuracy. The mastiff bounded to his feet as the rock struck the boards with a loud noise and ricocheted into some bushes. He stared at the spot and bared his teeth in a low growl. Then he trotted alertly toward the fence and nosed among the foliage.

Nancy stood poised on the balls of her feet, waiting until the dog had gone as far from the gate as his leash would permit. Then she darted forward, lifted the latch, and tugged at the gate.

The mastiff heard her and raced back with a fierce snarl. For a frightening instant, Nancy thought the gate would never open. Then it swung in, and she ran outside the enclosure a split second ahead of the dog!

Glancing over her shoulder, Nancy saw the dog lunge and paw the air as he came to the end of his leash. Angry barks filled the night. As Nancy dashed among the trees, she heard excited women's voices from the enclosure.

"Oh, I hope they don't let that beast loose!" Nancy said fervently.

In the darkness she could not at once determine the direction she should take but dared not pause.

"I must get away!" she told herself.

Running as rapidly as she could in the darkness, ducking under low-hanging branches, dodging around bushes, she suddenly stumbled onto a narrow dirt lane. It appeared to be the same one Nancy and the two cousins had found earlier. Assuming it must lead to the gravel road, Nancy followed the path thankfully.

But her relief was short-lived! Bright white beams of light began to flash among the trees a distance behind her.

Her pursuers had picked up her trail! With the advantage of light, they began to gain on her. Her breath coming fast, Nancy went on around a bend in the lane. She stopped short.

Coming toward her along the winding path was a car. Its high beam lights blinded her temporarily. The driver surely had seen her. Now there certainly was no chance of escape!

Suddenly a wild thought came to Nancy. Maybe this was unexpected aid! Perhaps the girls had fled from the mysterious woods to summon help.

Nancy stared at the car tensely. With a gentle squeal of brakes, it rolled to a stop. Its lights dimmed.

Was she to be rescued or captured?

CHAPTER XV

Hot on the Trail

NANCY stood frozen to the spot. Not a sound permeated the woods from the direction of the car.

Then from somewhere behind her came a woman's voice: "That dog must have opened the gate! You know he did it once before. We may as well go back."

Nancy was jubilant. The Lavender Sisters did not know she had been inside the enclosure! But there was still uncertainty ahead. Courageously she stood her ground to see what would happen down the lane. A moment later a small figure bounded out of the darkness.

"Togo!" Nancy exclaimed joyously, and she hurried forward. In a few moments she was joined by Bess, George, Dick Milton, and Hannah Gruen.

"Nancy! Nancy, are you all right?" Hannah whispered hoarsely.

She stopped breathlessly in front of Nancy and hugged her.

"Yes, I'm all right. But I'm certainly glad to see you."

"Hypers!" said George. "You sure scared us!"

"What happened?" Bess demanded.

Nancy told her story. She ended by telling Dick that despite her efforts, she had learned nothing new about the China clay pit.

"The important thing is that you're safe!" Hannah Gruen declared. "Now let's get out of here. I'm sure your father will be terribly upset when he hears about this!"

"Where is Dad?" Nancy asked.

"He received an urgent telephone call from Washington," Mrs. Gruen explained, "and caught the afternoon plane. He doesn't know how long he'll be gone."

Nancy nodded. She wondered if the lawyer's trip to Washington concerned the Engs. Her thoughts were interrupted by Bess.

"George and I couldn't imagine what in the world had happened to you in that enclosure," Bess said as they walked toward her car. "We waited and waited. When you didn't answer after I called, George was all for going inside to find you! Then your note came over the fence, and we didn't know what to think!"

"But we hid in the woods," George said, "just as you warned us to do."

"And not a second too soon, I can tell you!" Bess went on. "We'd hardly jumped behind a tree when that Lavender Sister came outside."

"What about the ladder?" Nancy queried, still curious. "Couldn't she see it?"

"We took the ladder away and hid it right after you let yourself down inside, since you said you were coming out the gate," George replied.

"When the woman opened the gate," Bess took up the story, "we saw that awful mastiff chained right inside the gate." She gave a slight shudder. "So we knew you *couldn't* get out!"

After the Lavender Sister had re-entered the enclosure, the cousins explained, they had hurried through the woods to Bess's car and driven to Nancy's home to get her father. Upon learning that the lawyer had left for Washington, Bess had telephoned Dick Milton and asked him to return with them. Hannah Gruen, upset and anxious, had announced that she and Togo would go along too.

"It's a good thing we found the lane earlier," George declared, "or we couldn't have got here so fast."

"And a good thing I took it," Nancy said ruefully, "or you'd have missed me!"

They got into Bess's car, turned on the narrow lane, and drove off. The headlights focused on Nancy's convertible, still parked in the small clearing. Mrs. Gruen had brought the spare ignition key.

Easing into the driver's seat, Nancy turned on the motor and listened to its sound with evident satisfaction. Mrs. Gruen climbed in beside her. Whistling to Togo to join them, Nancy put the car in gear and followed Bess toward home.

Both cars pulled up at a corner a few blocks from Bess's home. "Thanks a million!" Nancy called to her friends.

She waved, then drove straight on while Bess turned off toward Dick's house. A few minutes later Nancy swung the car into her driveway.

"That's strange!" Mrs. Gruen spoke in amazement. "I left the lights on in the living room and hall when I went out."

The windows were completely dark. Suddenly the terrier began to bark excitedly.

"What is it, Togo?" Nancy asked quickly.

She opened the door of the car and the dog jumped out. He dashed up the front steps and scratched at the door.

"He acts as if someone were in the house!" Hannah Gruen exclaimed.

Nancy nodded. "Go around to the back of the house. I'll take the front. If there *is* a burglar inside, maybe we can trap him."

"All right. But be careful, Nancy."

"I will. And you, too."

She waited until the housekeeper got to the rear yard, then she went up the front steps.

Togo barked as she set foot on the porch. Turning her key in the lock, Nancy opened the door, snapped on the hall light, and looked inside. Togo sniffed the floor, racing from one room to another. Nancy followed him. No one was around, and apparently nothing had been disturbed.

In the front hall Nancy was joined by Mrs. Gruen. "I didn't see a soul—" she began, then broke off as Nancy's fingers tightened on her arm.

From the second floor of the house came soft distinct sounds!

"Come on!" Nancy whispered.

She flicked a switch to turn on the upper hall lights, then cautiously ascended the stairs, followed by Mrs. Gruen. Togo went ahead of them.

Nancy had just snapped on a light in her own bedroom when the dog began to bark wildly down the hall. As she turned to go after him, she glanced at her dressing table. The drawer had been lifted out and its contents strewn on the floor! One look told Nancy that Mr. Soong's jade elephant was gone!

As she turned to search the other rooms for the intruder, a scream came from a rear bedroom.

Recognizing the distressed voice as Hannah'

Gruen's, Nancy ran to the back room. She found the housekeeper unhurt but staring wildly out the window.

"He went that way!" she cried, pointing toward the garden. "He jumped off the back-porch roof and disappeared over the hedge!"

Nancy ran downstairs with Togo in pursuit of the burglar. But her chase was fruitless. He had too much of a head start. Upon her return she asked the housekeeper what the man looked like.

"I'm afraid I didn't get a good look, Nancy," Mrs. Gruen confessed.

They searched the house. Nothing but the jade elephant was missing.

Nancy stood lost in thought. The man was no ordinary burglar or he would have stolen other things.

Who could the thief be? Manning-Carr?

Accompanied by Mrs. Gruen and Togo, Nancy went outside with a flashlight and examined the soft earth at the back porch.

She soon found the footprints she was seeking, deeply embedded in the ground from the force of the thief's jump. They looked like the same short, wide prints she had seen in the Townsends' flower bed after their vase had been stolen!

"I feel kind of fidgety," Mrs. Gruen remarked when they had returned to the house and made sure all the doors and windows were locked for the night.

Nancy called the police. She reported that she had recovered her car, then told of the theft of the jade elephant. As a routine matter they came and made an investigation. Then the young detective had a snack and wearily tumbled into bed.

Her waking thought was of Mr. Soong and she determined to go to his home at once to talk to him. Not only did she have the unpleasant task of telling him about the jade elephant, but she was eager to learn from him the meaning of the strange Oriental symbol she had copied from the leaning chimney.

As on previous visits, the door to Mr. Soong's house was opened by the servant Ching. His expressionless face spread into a smile when he saw Nancy and he made a deep bow.

"Is Mr. Soong at home?" Nancy asked.

The man shook his head.

Nancy deliberated a moment, then took a notebook from her purse and scribbled a short message asking Mr. Soong to call her at the house or after twelve-thirty at Dick Milton's home. This was the nineteenth, and she had promised to take care of Baby Sue.

She gave the message to Ching and he gesticulatingly promised to deliver it. Then he bowed smilingly and closed the door.

Nancy went back home to await Mr. Soong's call.

"I hope he hasn't gone out of town," she sighed. Just then the phone rang.

"Nancy Drew?" a voice boomed. "Come right over here!"

"Is this Mr. Monroe?" she asked.

"Sure is. And I believe I have a clue to the China clay pit to show you."

"What is it?"

The geologist refused to impart any further information over the telephone. Grabbing her handbag, Nancy explained her errand to Hannah Gruen, then drove off.

The tall, sharp-featured professor led Nancy into the living room in silence. Taking a package from his desk, he thrust it into her hands.

"What do you make of this?" he barked.

Nancy looked at the parcel. It had been sent from San Francisco and had obviously been unwrapped.

She studied the address. Painted in bold, black letters on gray paper were the words:

M. MONROE
GENERAL DELIVERY
RIVER HEIGHTS

Nancy looked questioningly at the geologist. "Open it!" he commanded.

She opened a white cardboard box inside the paper. Neatly packed in rows were several tubes of paint with Chinese markings.

"'This is the kind of paint that potters use!" Nancy exclaimed in surprise as she recalled similar tubes of paint at Dick Milton's workshop.

"It is!" Professor Monroe snorted. "And these tubes must have been shipped from China. Their colors are among the finest and purest I've seen! Only thing is," he added dramatically, "I didn't order them!"

"Who did then?" Nancy asked.

"I'll let you guess," the geologist answered.

"This package must have been meant for the other Miles Monroe!" she exclaimed. "The man who owns the tract of land near Hunter's Creek!"

"Precisely!" the professor boomed, and his eyes sparkled. "And why would our mysterious friend have the paints sent to him unless he intended to use them on porcelain?"

Nancy tingled with rising excitement. She was convinced that the strange, fenced-in enclosure was near a pit of China clay. And someone was making pottery there!

"I'll take the package back to the post office," she told the geologist, "and stand watch until M. Monroe calls for it!"

"Good idea!" he barked. "Go to it!"

To herself Nancy said, "And I'll bet this other M. Monroe is Manning-Carr. Oh dear! I wish I hadn't promised I'd take care of Baby Sue today. There's no time to lose on this mystery."

But Nancy was a person of her word, and she

would not disappoint Connie Milton. She did decide, however, to call first Bess, then George, to ask them to help her out if something vital should develop. Using the geologist's telephone, she was told that both girls would be away until late afternoon.

"So I'm on my own this time," Nancy reflected, leaving the geologist's apartment.

When she arrived at the General Delivery window of the post office, she met with both disappointment and a surprise.

"M. Monroe was here only fifteen minutes ago!" the clerk informed Nancy as she handed him the parcel and explained the error. "He was plenty angry when I told him I had sent it to the professor!"

"Is Mr. Monroe an olive-skinned man with black hair and piercing black eyes?" she asked, giving the clerk a description of Manning-Carr.

The clerk shook his head decisively. "The man I talked to," he said, "was Chinese."

"Chinese!" she exclaimed. "What did he look like?"

The clerk stared at her helplessly. "Why, uh— like a Chinaman!" he replied.

Nancy bit her lip in vexation.

"Wait a minute, miss. I just remembered something! That Chinese said he was going to hunt up the other Miles Monroe and get his package!"

CHAPTER XVI

The Riddle Unravels

"THANKS a lot!" Nancy cried to the postal clerk.

She dashed off to a telephone booth in a nearby store. Within a few seconds she had the professor on the wire. Learning that no Chinese had been there, Nancy told him to be on guard.

Miles Monroe thanked her for warning him.

Feeling confident that the Oriental was probably the same one who had collected the money orders in Masonville under Mr. Soong's name, she put a call through to her friend Chief McGinnis.

Quickly the young detective voiced her suspicions. "And I'm sure he's Manning-Carr's brother."

The officer thought her clue a very important one. "I'll put a man on duty at the professor's place right away," he told her.

Nancy quickly hurried to her car. She was due at Connie Milton's. She hoped Mr. Soong had telephoned the Drew home by now and that Hannah Gruen had told him where he could reach her.

"Go onto the party and have a good time!" she told Connie when she arrived.

Connie thanked Nancy, and left. Nancy played with Sue for a few minutes, then placed the cooing infant in the carriage on the porch. Watching until she saw the baby's eyes slowly close, she tiptoed quietly into the house.

Nancy tried to read, but her mind was too full of the mystery. Finally she put aside the book and concentrated on her sketch of the iron ornament on the leaning chimney.

"Maybe the answer to the whole puzzle is in this," she mused.

When four o'clock came and she had not heard from Mr. Soong, Nancy could not check her mounting curiosity any longer. She went to the telephone and dialed his number. The call was answered immediately by the Chinese importer himself.

"I left a note for you to phone me!" Nancy told him.

"I'm afraid I don't understand."

"Didn't Ching give you my note?"

"Ching is not here," Mr. Soong replied. "He must have put the message in his pocket."

Nancy said that she had something important to show Mr. Soong, and he promised to hurry over at once. When he arrived, Nancy told him first of her recent experience inside the enclosure, then showed him her sketch of the iron ornament. Mr. Soong's eyebrows lifted in surprise.

"It is a Chinese symbol," he stated, confirming Nancy's deduction. "It means 'help'!"

" 'Help'?" Nancy repeated.

"Yes." Mr. Soong took a pen from his pocket and printed a word on the back of an envelope. "If it could be written in English, the word would be spelled like this."

"Phang?" Nancy said haltingly.

"That is just the way the word is spelled. It is pronounced *bong*."

Nancy stared at him in sudden excitement.

"*Bong?* You mean that's a cry for help?"

Mr. Soong nodded.

"I heard such a sound come from near the enclosure!" Nancy announced triumphantly. "A scream that sounded exactly like *bong!*"

Mr. Soong was so mystified Nancy hastily apprised him of everything she now suspected.

First, she said the enclosure was not merely a religious retreat. With or without the knowledge of the Lavender Sisters, the valuable clay was being dug up on the property.

"I heard a motor working last night," she said. "They probably dig only when outsiders aren't likely to be around."

Second, Nancy reviewed the double puzzle of

the stolen and faked potteries. The rare old pieces, including Mr. Soong's prized Ming vase which had been stolen by a thief known as John Manning; the clever imitations of valuable old potteries, which had been sold by a man named Carr; and the supposition that Manning and Carr were the same person, and used other aliases, perhaps Monroe among them.

Third, Nancy told the importer of finding her missing car near the enclosure. Since the car had been stolen by the person who had dropped the jade elephant by the stream, it looked as if he were associated with the pottery thieves.

Mr. Soong listened intently. "My dear," he said, "your powers of deduction contain the wisdom of a Chinese philosopher."

"I'm only putting two and two together," she replied modestly.

Then, last of all, Nancy brought up the subject of Eng Moy and his daughter Eng Lei. Both had vanished mysteriously in the company of a man known as David Carr. Eng Moy's signature had appeared on at least two of the pottery pieces, which were clever imitations.

"I believe," said Nancy, "that your friends are mixed up with this Carr in the fake pottery making. No doubt they are not willing partners. They may be the prisoners in that enclosure!"

Mr. Soong gave a start, then sat for a moment without speaking.

"I know how damaging the facts must appear. But when the truth is out, I believe in my heart that Eng Moy and Lei will be found to be innocent of any wrongdoing," he said with simple dignity.

Nancy leaned forward. "To save them from further harm, I believe we should notify the police at once," she said.

"Oh, no!" the Chinese cried out. "Please!"

"If that place in the woods contains criminals, it's our duty to notify the authorities."

The Chinese wrung his hands. "For the sake of my good friends," he pleaded, "don't tell the police now. Please give the Engs a chance to clear their names before they are arrested."

Then he hung his head. "If there were only some way—" He looked at Nancy. "Would you show me the path to the leaning chimney?" he asked pathetically. "I must find out the truth about my friends! Those wretches may kill Moy and Lei so they cannot talk. Please, Miss Drew."

Nancy was touched by the man's sincerity. "You're a real friend," she said. "I'll help you."

"You'll show me the way to the enclosure?"

"Yes," Nancy promised.

"When?"

"Soon! Here comes Mrs. Milton."

When Nancy told Connie Milton where they were going, the young woman strongly objected. But upon being told the trip was only an investigation prior to calling the police, she felt better.

"Dick has something in the cellar you might use to get over the wall," Connie told Nancy. "It's a rope ladder with metal grappling hooks."

Nancy was delighted to have it, since she was not certain the ladder Bess and George had hidden in the woods was still there. In any case, it would have been too heavy to lift over the board fence and to use as a means of escape.

Nancy thanked Connie, put the rope ladder into her car, and set off with Mr. Soong. It was already late afternoon when they arrived at the part of the grounds where the leaning chimney was. Nancy wanted to show him the ornament. Walking to the little knoll from which it could be seen, she exclaimed:

"The Phang ornament! It's gone!"

It was possible that the person who had put up the symbol had not wanted the Lavender Sisters to know about it. And Nancy remembered she had mentioned it to one of the women!

Quickly she attached the hooks of the rope ladder to the fence, breaking the rusted barbed wire, climbed up, and looked over. With no one in sight in the weed-filled garden, it seemed safe for her and Mr. Soong to drop down inside.

The elderly gentleman was more agile than she had supposed and dropped lightly to the ground behind her. She hid the ladder beneath a bush and said, pointing:

"We're in luck!"

The wooden door in the stone wall which ran from the old brick building to the fence stood open! Cautiously Nancy and Mr. Soong went through. Then, keeping in the shelter of the many trees, she led the way to the area where she had seen lights and heard the engine.

They encountered no one but heard muffled thuds. Presently they reached the spot. The sight ahead of them made Nancy's heart beat faster.

There was a shallow pit of sand-colored earth and flintlike layers of rock. Two Chinese, wearing mud-spattered overalls, stood ankle-deep in the pit, breaking up the rock with sledge hammers. Another man scooped up the yellowish soil with a shovel, while a fourth workman carried away the soil and broken pieces of shale in a wheelbarrow.

To Nancy the rocks had the hard, gray look of granite, and she turned to Mr. Soong to confirm her observation.

"There's kaolin in it?" she whispered.

Mr. Soong bobbed his head excitedly. "A high percentage. Excellent for making porcelain."

But Nancy did not allow her elation to overshadow the main reason for her coming to the secret spot. She must still hunt for the Engs.

"Come on!" she whispered. Keeping well hidden, Nancy led Mr. Soong from one part of the grounds to another, hoping, with each step, that the huge mastiff would not appear.

They passed a small bungalow and several pitched tents but saw no one. Finally Nancy concluded that probably the Lavender Sisters and any others in the enclosure besides the diggers must be inside the mysterious building.

"We'll go back there," she told Mr. Soong.

Reaching the brick building with the leaning chimney, Mr. Soong stared at it hopefully.

The door was closed, and the small dust-covered windows were much too high for anyone to look inside. There were no sounds from within.

"We'll go closer," Nancy said.

As she stepped forward, the door suddenly swung back and a slender, pretty Chinese girl about Nancy's age appeared. She wore a clay-spattered canvas apron over a plain gray cotton dress.

The girl stood for a moment, looking at the pit, then suddenly burst into sobs.

"That may be Eng Lei!" Nancy thought.

A man came through the doorway and put his arm soothingly around the girl's shoulder. He spoke to her softly in Chinese.

Mr. Soong's fingers suddenly closed tightly over Nancy's wrist and she saw as she turned that his eyes were fixed excitedly on the man.

"It is my friend!" he whispered. "Eng Moy!"

He started forward, but Nancy held him back. "Before we show ourselves, we must find out what his position is here and be sure that he won't betray us," she whispered.

For a moment Mr. Soong looked upset, then he smiled. "My heart is so full of the desire to greet my old friend," he said apologetically, "I am afraid my head is forgetful. I will try to be more careful."

Nancy pressed his arm reassuringly as she studied the middle-aged Eng Moy. Coarse blue-denim work clothes, splashed with white clay, hung loosely on his thin, frail body. His face, as he spoke comfortingly to the girl, showed a quiet resignation that told of long suffering.

"The girl must be Eng Lei," Nancy murmured to Mr. Soong, her heart going out to the old gentleman as his eyes reflected the tension under which he was laboring.

He nodded eagerly. "I think you are right. But so many years have passed since I last saw Lei—she was only a child when I left China many years ago—I cannot be sure."

"What are they saying?" Nancy whispered as Eng Moy again spoke softly to the girl in Chinese.

Mr. Soong shook his head. "I cannot hear," he confessed.

A moment later the Engs turned back into the building. Nancy and Mr. Soong stole swiftly and cautiously through the entrance after them.

CHAPTER XVII

Reunion

THE room in which Nancy and Mr. Soong found themselves was small and dimly lighted. It contained nothing but a few crates stacked near a doorway. The two eavesdroppers hid behind them. Beyond was a large, better-lighted room. In this a wide workbench was arranged along one wall. On it lay tubes of paint and bowls of turpentine containing brushes.

Lined along the rear of the workbench were two neat rows of porcelain bowls, jugs, jars and vases, all glazed and beautifully decorated with Oriental designs. Above them on the wall were cabinets, their doors closed.

Eng Moy and his daughter Lei took their places at the workbench, their backs to the door. They picked up the delicate designing brushes and began working on two gracefully shaped potteries.

"Look at the vase Eng Moy just took from the cabinet!" Nancy whispered.

"Why, it's mine!" Mr. Soong whispered excitedly. "The vase stolen from Milton's shop!"

"Exactly," confirmed Nancy. "And if you look closely, you'll see why Manning-Carr wanted it. Eng Moy is copying it—and probably made the copy which Manning-Carr sold in New York."

At that moment the Lavender Sister who had ordered Nancy away from the enclosure some days before entered the room through a far doorway. She gave the Engs a hostile glance, then bent to examine their work. Suddenly she pointed to a small jar and uttered a stream of Chinese.

Stepping swiftly toward Lei, before the father could intervene, she slapped the girl's face. Then she turned abruptly and departed through the same doorway from which she had appeared.

Nancy caught a fleeting glimpse of the interior beyond, containing pottery-making equipment.

As the door closed, Nancy heard the sound of weeping. Once more Eng Moy attempted to comfort his daughter, but she resisted his soothing words.

Mr. Soong, listening to the exchange of Chinese, translated it to Nancy:

"Father, I cannot stand this hateful life any longer!" Lei sobbed. "I wish I had never been born!"

"You must not talk that way, my child," Eng Moy remonstrated gently. "You are too young to give up hope."

"Hope!" the girl replied bitterly. "Day after day, year after year I have lived because of that word! Hoping for rescue! Hoping for the capture and punishment of the men who keep us here! Hoping to see China and home again! I tell you, Father, it is no use! Hope for us is an empty word. I never want to hear it again!"

His face eloquent with distress, Eng Moy turned away. "But what can we do?"

"We have only one choice left, Father," Lei told him. "We must end it all, rather than spend our lives in misery. It is our only means of escape."

"No! Never that!" Mr. Soong cried out in Chinese.

He came from behind the crates and went quickly toward the Engs, followed by Nancy. Surprise flashed across Lei's face, then she backed away in sudden fear.

Mr. Soong went directly to Eng Moy and embraced him. "My friend! My old friend!" he murmured.

Eng Moy drew back and stared at the old gentleman. Then slowly a look of recognition dawned. "Soong!" he whispered disbelievingly.

He blinked in bewilderment, as if unable to

credit what he saw. Then he stepped forward with a happy cry and returned Mr. Soong's embrace.

Introductions quickly followed. Smiling proudly at Nancy, Mr. Soong spoke rapidly to the Engs. When he had finished, they turned to Nancy, their faces reflecting gratitude and hope.

Eng Moy took Nancy's hands in his and addressed her haltingly in Chinese, while Lei smiled in agreement.

Despite the barrier of languages—for the Engs could neither speak nor understand English—Nancy and the Chinese father and daughter became friends at once.

"What are they trying to tell me?" Nancy asked.

"They wish to thank you for bringing me here," Mr. Soong replied.

"There'll be enough time for that when we're all safely out of the enclosure," Nancy said. "We must hurry away before we're caught!"

Nancy had Mr. Soong explain her plan, whereby all four of them would climb over the fence where she and her companion had hidden the ladder. The Engs nodded eagerly to show Nancy they understood.

Leading the way to the door, Nancy pulled it open a crack and cautiously peered outside. A second later she caught her breath.

Coming toward the old brick building was a man with black hair and dark skin. But the most striking thing about him was his eyes. They seemed to stare from his head like two glittering black marbles. Nancy, though she had never met him, was sure she knew his identity.

The Engs' reply to Mr. Soong's inquiry confirmed her suspicion. The man was David Carr! Nancy closed the door quickly.

"Tell the Engs they must hide us!" Nancy said.

Eng Moy and Lei looked stunned at the turn of events.

"Let's take a chance on that room beyond," Nancy suggested quickly.

Eng Moy said he would run ahead and see if anyone were in it. He reported two women were at work there.

Nancy glanced through the window. Carr had stopped to inspect something on the ground. A moment's grace.

"Ask the Engs if they can let us have some old work clothes, Mr. Soong," she instructed. "We'll take a chance getting past those women."

The Chinese quickly translated. Hurrying to a row of hooks jutting from the wall, Lei brought back a clay-spattered apron for Nancy and a similarly messy pair of overalls for Mr. Soong.

"Hurry!" Nancy said to him. "Carr may come in here any minute!"

"Let's hope we avoid detection," Nancy whispered

They swiftly slipped the garments over their own clothing and Nancy wound a scarf around her head.

"Let's hope we avoid detection," she whispered to Mr. Soong.

She opened the door to the workshop. Then, taking a deep breath, she stepped into the shop and started along the shadowy wall toward the opposite end of the room where there was still another door.

Nancy walked as casually as she could, her face slightly averted from the women, who stood at tables pounding clay. After a moment Nancy noted gratefully that Lei had slipped up beside her to help screen her from suspicious stares. Behind her were Eng Moy and Mr. Soong.

Two or three times the women workers looked up at them curiously but showed no signs of suspecting anything amiss. At last the four arrived at the end of the shop.

Going through a doorway into a short corridor, Nancy saw a large iron door. The Engs whispered something and Mr. Soong translated for Nancy.

"Behind the door is a brick vault containing genuine old Chinese porcelains, all of them stolen," he explained. "Only Carr and his brother possess keys to the vault."

Nancy felt a twinge of excitement. The mystery was unraveling fast now! And this was the first real evidence that the swindler's brother was working with him!

The group had stopped, safe for the moment. Then terror struck their hearts. Outside the wall where the four were huddled the horrible mastiff began to bay.

Had an alarm been given?

CHAPTER XVIII

Meeting the Enemy

ESCAPE was now impossible.

"Our only chance is to hide until the dog is taken away," Nancy said to Mr. Soong. "Ask your friends if there's a place where we can wait without too much risk of being detected."

Eng Moy led them to a small room at the extreme rear corner of the building. He pointed to a battered old brick wall.

Walking to the end of it, Eng Moy pulled open a rusty iron door. As it creaked back on rusty hinges, he stepped into a dank, dark cavern and lighted a candle. Then, turning, he motioned to the others to follow.

Nancy exclaimed in surprise. They were standing in a large, dome-shaped area about eight feet high at the center. The circular brick wall was dilapidated and battered, and the rough stone flooring cracked. Nancy noticed that the roof of the oven funneled into the leaning chimney.

"This must have been the smelter of the old iron mine!" she told Mr. Soong excitedly.

The elderly gentleman spoke a few words to Eng Moy.

"You are right, my dear," he reported. "When Eng Moy came to the enclosure, this old smelter was used as a kiln to fire pottery. But it seemed as if the chimney might topple over, so a modern kiln was constructed across the garden."

Lei went off to stand watch at the far door, to give notice the instant anyone might come along the corridor. Nancy, Eng Moy, and Mr. Soong sat down on the floor to await a favorable time to escape. As they marked time, the pottery maker haltingly told his friend all that had happened to him and his daughter since they had arrived in San Francisco five years before.

Eng Moy said that the man known to him as David Carr had been a business acquaintance in China. He had tricked the Engs into coming to America by making the father promises of an important position in one of the country's modern pottery plants. As the final stop in their tour of United States factories, Carr had lured them to the enclosure in the woods, and there made them prisoners.

The Engs had lived in captivity four and a half

years. During that time they had been forced to make fake Chinese porcelains, using as their models genuine, rare old Oriental pieces that Carr had stolen.

"But didn't the Engs ever try to escape?" Nancy asked.

Mr. Soong translated her question, then turned back to the girl.

"Yes, many times," he told Nancy. "Twice they even reached the woods outside the board fence before their absence was discovered. But the dog soon found them, and their poor bodies still bear the marks of the whip Carr used to punish them."

Nancy's ire was aroused anew. Poor Lei and her father had been the victims of extreme cruelty.

"Then it was Lei I heard scream for help?" Nancy asked. "The cry that sounded like *bong?*"

"Yes," Mr. Soong answered. "The two Phang characters you saw attached to the chimney also were appeals for help. Eng Moy put them there, hoping to attract someone's attention. He shaped the characters out of old scraps of iron he found."

"That, of course, is why Eng took down the old ornament," Nancy observed. "But who removed the new one?"

"My friend was compelled to remove it the day he put it up," Mr. Soong said. "One of the Lavender Sisters saw it and punished him."

Nancy's conscience pricked her. *She* had told

the woman about it and no doubt caused this punishment! Quickly Nancy had Mr. Soong explain this and offered her regrets.

"Eng Moy says he is so glad you saw it, the offense does not matter," Mr. Soong translated. "The clue of the leaning chimney is the means of your finding him and Lei."

Nancy was told that Eng Moy's signature, cunningly worked into the designs of various pieces of pottery, had also been intended by him as an appeal for aid.

Carr had made sure his prisoners were given no opportunity to learn English. Knowing that government authorities would be trying to locate him for illegally remaining in the United States, Eng Moy hoped one of the signatures would come to the attention of Federal officers and lead them to the enclosure.

"Are the other people," Nancy said suddenly, "those men and women we saw working in the pit and in the shop, prisoners too?"

Mr. Soong put the question to Eng Moy.

"The men are foreigners," Mr. Soong translated the answer. "The women are their wives. Carr and his brother smuggled them into the United States by plane. He promised them wonderful things, then he made them prisoners. Finally he threatened if they did not dig the clay and operate the machines, he would expose them and have them put in jail for life!"

At that moment they heard the iron door squeak open. Lei slipped into the candlelit smelter. She spoke breathlessly to her father and from the sudden fear that flitted across his face Nancy knew something had gone wrong.

"The Engs' absence has been discovered!" Mr. Soong told her with alarm. "Carr and the woman are out in the corridor!"

Motioning to the others to wait, Nancy stole from the old smelter into the shadowy room outside and listened.

"You fool!" cried a man's voice. "If you'd paid more attention to the Engs, they couldn't have disappeared!"

"They can't have gone far!" the Lavender Sister replied.

"Get the dog," Carr said shortly. "She and that father of hers are probably in the smelter room. My mastiff will attend to them!"

Nancy turned and ran softly back to the smelter. "They're coming!" she whispered.

Eng Moy blew out the candle, and the four waited with mounting suspense in the dark. Then, after an interval that seemed to be years, a voice spoke sharply in Chinese outside the iron door.

"It is Carr!" Mr. Soong whispered fearfully to Nancy. "He demands that the Engs come out! What shall we do?" he asked in panic.

Before she could reply that it would be best for them to slip out without betraying her and

Mr. Soong's presence, the door was pulled open.

Carr stepped into the doorway and shone a flashlight about. When he saw Nancy and Mr. Soong, his thin lips spread in a slow, mocking smile.

"So! I have caught you at last!" he said sarcastically.

The Lavender Sister, who arrived with the mastiff, gave a dry, harsh chuckle when she saw Nancy.

"Take the Engs away and make sure they do not try to escape again," her husband ordered.

The woman beckoned sharply. With a despairing glance at Nancy and Mr. Soong, the Engs followed Carr's wife through the doorway.

Nancy watched them go with a heavy heart. How happy they had been when freedom seemed so near, she reflected. And how utterly defeated they now appeared.

Carr studied Nancy and her companion silently, then spoke again in a cold, sharp voice. "I intend to do away with you two before any of your friends can get here to help you!"

CHAPTER XIX

Escape

AT David Carr's harsh words, Mr. Soong moaned.

"Nobody," Carr shouted angrily, "is going to interfere with me and get away with it! You, Nancy Drew, have interfered with my plans since the first time you saw me on Three Bridges Road."

"And I'll keep on interfering—until you and your brother are locked behind bars!" Nancy retorted.

Carr's face tightened. "Ah! So you know about my brother?"

"I do!" Nancy declared, hoping it would induce the swindler to reveal what part his brother had played in Carr's nefarious schemes.

Instead, Carr said, "You are very clever. Since you probably know it, I'll admit he stole the vase from the Townsends and the jade elephant from your home."

162

Nancy nodded. "Why did he bother to steal the vase when he knew it was a fake?"

"My wife is to blame for that!" he replied harshly. "Because of her stupidity, Eng Moy was able to paint his name on several porcelains I sold. My brother and I stole back as many as we could. We were afraid the signature would be traced by Federal dicks."

"You managed to remove Eng's name and sold the Townsend vase again. But who posed as Mr. Soong to collect the money orders in Masonville?" she asked quickly, hoping to catch Carr off guard. "Your brother?"

The man was much too cagey, however, to refer to his confederate by name. He addressed his reply tauntingly to the elderly Chinese gentleman, who stood listening close by.

"That was clever, eh, Soong? It's just too bad for Miss Drew his scheme didn't completely succeed. If she'd believed you guilty of selling fake potteries, she might have stopped meddling in my affairs and wouldn't be here now to face the consequences!"

"I'm glad I was able to help Mr. Soong," Nancy declared hotly.

Carr gave a mirthless, sardonic laugh, then turned to go. "I advise you not to try to escape," he warned. "The mastiff has a nasty temper and very sharp fangs! I'll be back in a few minutes and then we'll see how brave you are!"

He swung the iron door shut. Nancy found the candle and lighted it. She turned to Mr. Soong who had sat down on the floor, too weak to stand any longer.

"It's my fault you're in this dangerous situation," he murmured to Nancy. "I shouldn't have asked you to come with me."

Nancy smiled wanly. "Please do not feel bad. It was my own wish to untangle this mystery that brought us here."

She crossed to the door to listen, hoping the dog might be gone. But the mastiff outside, sensing her presence near the iron barrier, uttered a low, menacing growl.

Nancy took the candle and started to examine the battered brick walls. There *had* to be some way of escape!

Suddenly the iron door creaked slowly open. Standing in the doorway was Mr. Soong's short, inscrutable-looking servant Ching! He regarded them impassively, then gave them a toothy smile.

"Ching!" Mr. Soong arose and advanced toward him eagerly. He spoke excitedly to the servant in Chinese. But Ching suddenly gave a boisterous laugh and roughly pushed his gentle employer away.

"Fool!" he cried in English. "Are you so stupid you cannot guess who I really am?"

"Carr's brother!" Nancy exclaimed.

Ching made her a mock bow. "Exactly!"

"Now I understand several things," Nancy said. "You were the one who posed as Mr. Soong and cashed the money orders!"

"Yes, Miss Drew," Ching replied mockingly. "But my impersonation need not concern you any longer. You made a fatal mistake in coming here. Now you must pay for your stupidity." He chuckled contemptuously. "There is an old American saying, 'Curiosity killed the cat.' You see the parallel, Miss Drew, I'm sure."

"There's no use threatening us. You know my father will come and bring the police!" Nancy burst out.

"Wouldn't you like us to believe that, Miss Drew?" Ching taunted. "But unfortunately for you, I know that your father is in Washington. You see, I called his office, intending to tell him that you would be—er—slightly late for dinner."

Nancy realized how serious her plight was, but there was a ray of hope. When she did not return to dinner, Mrs. Gruen certainly would telephone the Miltons, and when the housekeeper learned that Nancy and Mr. Soong had gone to the enclosure, she would call the police.

Sparring for time, she continued to ask questions which Ching freely answered.

He said it had been prearranged between David and himself that he would get a job at Mr. Soong's. In this way he could watch the man's mail and waylay any messages about the Engs. At all times he kept track of his employer's movements.

"But once you slipped," Nancy spoke up. "A letter about the Engs did reach Mr. Soong."

"Unfortunately, yes. Then you came into the case, Miss Drew. But you shall never bother my brother or me again. As soon as we have removed our valuable property," Ching said defiantly, "we will come back and dynamite the leaning chimney. When it collapses, it will crush the roof of the smelter." He paused significantly. "Your fate will not be pleasant. But let us hope the end will be swift!"

For several seconds after Ching had departed, Nancy and Mr. Soong were too dazed even to talk. It occurred to Nancy that Mrs. Gruen would not be concerned about her absence until the dinner hour. The housekeeper would act promptly then, but it might be too late. Desperately Nancy began to try to figure some way out of their dreadful plight.

"There isn't a chance of escaping through the door with the mastiff on guard," she pointed out.

Holding the candle above her head, Nancy stared at the domelike roof of the old smelter. The opening which funneled into the leaning chimney was about two feet in diameter. Through the opening she could just see a patch of sunlit sky. A thought clicked and she turned excitedly to Mr. Soong.

"Didn't Eng Moy get up the inside of the chimney to attach the iron symbol?" she asked.

"Yes. He said he used a ladder and went up from here," the elderly gentleman replied.

There was no ladder in the smelter. Nancy again peered up the chimney. Ladder or no ladder, she promptly decided to try the climb.

"Please help me get up," she said.

Mr. Soong's eyes widened. "You don't intend to climb the chimney?" he asked in alarm.

"I must!" Nancy told him. "It's our only chance of escape."

"But you might slip and fall!"

"Nothing would be worse than the fate that awaits us here," Nancy pointed out. "But if I can make the climb, I may be able to bring help to you and your friends before it's too late."

Recognizing that there was no choice, the Chinese, exerting his last ounce of strength, permitted Nancy to stand on his back so she could reach into the opening. As Nancy pulled herself up inside, Mr. Soong looked at her anxiously.

"Be careful," he begged. "If anything should happen to you—"

"Please don't worry," Nancy reassured him. "And don't give up hope. If everything goes well, I'll be back with the police."

"Good fortune go with you!" said Mr. Soong, sinking to the floor.

Nancy began her climb. Bracing her back

against one side of the chimney and her legs against the other, she started to inch up the stack.

Her climb was made easier by the angle at which the chimney slanted. But the cement between the bricks was chipped and broken. With every movement she made, Nancy was in danger of dislodging a loose brick and plunging down the dank shaft to the floor of the smelter!

With utmost care, she crept upward. Finally, when it seemed as if her tense, tired muscles could carry her no farther, she reached the top. Then she climbed carefully down the outside of the leaning chimney to the sloping roof of the old brick building.

She was about to make the drop from the edge of the roof to the garden when she heard a noise.

"Someone's coming!" she thought with alarm.

Swiftly Nancy flattened herself against the sloping roof, and a moment later saw Carr's wife, now in street clothes, open the door in the stone wall and walk in her direction.

As long as the woman did not look up, Nancy knew she was safe from view. But the angle at which the roof sloped made her position precarious. As Carr's wife approached, Nancy's grip suddenly weakened and she started to slide down.

"I can't fail now!" she told herself desperately. "I just can't!"

CHAPTER XX

A Fitting Reward

FRANTICALLY Nancy pressed her hands harder against the roof, and just when it seemed she must tumble to the ground, her momentum stopped.

Carr's wife paused to listen, but evidently did not detect the sound as coming from the roof. Finally she returned to the door in the stone wall and went through.

Nancy breathed with relief. Landing lightly on the spongy turf below the roof, she ran to where she had hidden the rope ladder. It was still there. Hooking the ladder to the top of the wooden fence, Nancy climbed over quickly.

She tossed the ladder behind a tree and ran headlong. Taking a circuitous route to avoid detection, she finally came to the parked car. She drove as swiftly as possible along the gravel lane; then sped toward Three Bridges Road. Crossing the intersection not twenty feet in front of her was the familiar car of a state trooper!

Nancy blew a long blast on her horn and the police car stopped. She slipped out of the convertible and ran toward the trooper.

"Thank goodness you're here!" she told him. "I need help—right away!"

"What's wrong, miss?"

Nancy apprised him of the situation.

"Looks as if we'll need plenty of help," the trooper said grimly.

He radioed his district headquarters, and after a short wait they were joined by six state troopers in a patrol car. With Nancy leading the way, they sped toward the enclosure.

The men went over the fence at various locations to make their roundup complete. Nancy and two of the officers went at once to the old brick building to free Mr. Soong.

None of the criminals was in sight, but some of the workers were arrested. Since none of them could speak English, they could tell the police nothing about Carr and his brother.

"You'll have an ugly dog to tackle in a minute," Nancy warned the troopers as they went on toward the old smelter.

"We'll take care of him."

To Nancy's surprise the mastiff was gone. Nancy was puzzled. What of Mr. Soong? She darted to the door of the smelter and yanked it open. The place was empty.

"He's been taken away!" she cried despairingly.

The troopers looked at her. Had they come too late?

Nancy had a sudden inspiration. "I believe I know where everybody is," she said.

She led the men to the large corridor vault where Eng Moy had said the valuable potteries were locked up. As Nancy expected, the door would not open, but she could detect a faint whine from within. She told the men she suspected the criminals and their mastiff were inside.

"Come out of there at once!" one of the troopers commanded.

There was utter silence. Suddenly Nancy realized that if her Chinese friends were inside with the criminals, they might be afraid to answer. So she called loudly:

"It's Nancy Drew! I've come with help!"

From inside came a cry of joy from Eng Lei, but it was stifled at once. The troopers said they would batter down the door if it were not opened immediately!

At last from the interior of the vault, their faces sullen, came Carr holding the dog by the leash, his wife, and Ching. Behind them were Mr. Soong and the Engs, who blinked happily.

The story was soon told. When Carr had discovered Nancy gone, he had rounded up his wife and brother to make a getaway. But Nancy had arrived with the police too soon. By hiding in the vault, Carr had hoped to make the group think he and Ching and the others already had left.

Before leaving, the Carrs would have disposed of the old Chinese and his friends. The workers outside did not know enough to give damaging evidence against the brothers.

"You meddlesome creature!" Carr's wife burst out, pointing a finger at Nancy. "You're to blame for our capture! In another year we would have become rich enough to leave this place forever. But you had to come snooping and spoil it all!"

At that moment another of the troopers approached to report that all the workers in the place had been captured. Nancy quickly introduced Mr. Soong, who was allowed to go. All the others would have to be held for questioning, the officer said, but he was sure the Engs would be allowed to stay at Mr. Soong's home.

"Tell Eng Moy and Eng Lei good-by for me, Mr. Soong, please," Nancy said with a smile.

"But you will see them again," the old importer promised. "They will not return to China at once."

The next day Mr. Drew, back from Washington, and thankful his daughter was safe, talked over the mystery with Nancy. The Carrs and

Ching, they learned from the police, had signed a complete confession.

"One of the things I'm most curious about," Mr. Drew remarked, "is how Carr and Ching obtained possession of the enclosure."

Nancy showed her father a copy of the confession. It said the discoverer of the kaolin had been the brothers' great-grandfather. His son had worked the pit for a while but had moved away. Then his son, the father of David and Ching, had gone to China as a merchant, and the property had been sold for taxes but never used.

Records, testifying to the existence and location of the pit, had lain untouched in Shanghai for many years. Then, five years ago, David Carr and his brother had found the records and had immediately come to the United States to look over the pit. Using the name of the geologist Miles Monroe, to avoid suspicion, Carr had purchased the tract of land, despite the fact that it did not have a clear title.

"Here's something interesting," Nancy said.

The Carrs had later learned that a man named Petersen had left papers which might upset their claim to the pit. David had been given a lead to the former owner of Mrs. Wendell's house in Masonville, and this was the telephone conversation Dick Milton had overheard six months ago.

Carr, using the name Manning, had gone to her

home, taken a room, and stolen the papers he wanted, as Nancy had guessed. He had installed the secret panel leading to the empty attic next door, to keep some of the valuable potteries there, in case the enclosure in the woods was raided.

"You spiked that one early in the game, Nancy." Mr. Drew grinned. "And you figured all along that the religious colony was just a camouflage."

"Well, in a way, the discovery of the leaning chimney in Masonville was a lucky coincidence." Nancy smiled. "If I hadn't found that, I might not have uncovered the secret of the enclosure."

A week later Mr. Soong held a party in honor of the Engs. Nancy and Mr. Drew were there, as well as Bess and George, Dick and Connie, and Ned Nickerson.

Nancy noted with satisfaction that displayed on the living-room mantel were Mr. Soong's jade elephant and the dragon Ming vase which had been recovered from the swindlers.

After dinner Mr. Soong made a short, touching speech expressing the debt of gratitude he and the Engs owed Nancy. Then Lei stepped forward, holding in her hands an exquisite vase.

Against a soft-green background was pictured a slender, golden-haired girl, pitting a lance at a scaly green dragon. Behind her stood a Chinese girl and two men in long Oriental robes.

As Lei presented the vase to a surprised Nancy with a warm smile, she spoke in Chinese.

"What is she saying?" Nancy asked Mr. Soong.

"Lei is trying to tell you that she and her father made this for you. Like all Chinese work, the design tells a story," he explained. "The girl is Nancy Drew. The three Chinese are Lei, Moy, and myself whom you are protecting from the evil dragon: Ching, Carr, and his wife."

He turned the vase bottom up. "It says, 'Made in the hearts of Eng Moy and Eng Lei.'"

"It's lovely," she whispered. "Thank you," Nancy said simply. "Thank you very much."

She started to turn away, but there was a burst of applause from the smiling circle of guests.

"Speech!" George prompted, spurring the others to even greater hand clapping.

Nancy looked helplessly at Mr. Soong. "Please do," he urged, smiling.

"Go ahead, Nancy," Ned spoke up.

"I'll do my best," she promised with a little laugh. "There aren't any words to express the way I feel about this vase. It's more to me than just a gift. It's a token of friendship; a bond between me and three of the nicest people I've ever known. I'll treasure it always."

Applause burst out again as she finished, then

the circle broke up and Nancy found herself in one corner of the room with Bess, George, and Ned.

"Well, Nancy," Ned said with a teasing grin, "now that you've located the China clay and the missing Engs, what are you going to do next?"

"Next," Nancy replied, "I'm going to tell you a secret. Mr. Soong is lending Dick the money to acquire the China clay, and the Engs are going to stay in America—for a while at least—and work with him making potteries. And now," she added, laughing, "I'm ready and willing to take on any new mystery that comes along."

Although Nancy did not know it then, the mystery was to be the baffling, exciting adventure of *The Secret of the Wooden Lady*.

"Meanwhile," Nancy whispered to Bess, "I think I'll join you in the ceramics class. Now that I've learned from Ching and Carr what *not* to do in making potteries, I'd better take a few tips from Dick on what *to* do!"

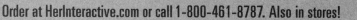

Match Wits with The Hardy Boys®!

Collect the Complete
Hardy Boys Mystery Stories®
by Franklin W. Dixon

The Hardy Boys Back-to-Back
#1: The Tower Treasure/#2: The House on the Cliff

Celebrate over 70 Years with the World's Greatest Super Sleuths!

Match Wits with Super Sleuth Nancy Drew!

Collect the Complete
Nancy Drew Mystery Stories®
by Carolyn Keene

Celebrate over 70 years with the World's Best Detective!